A Passion for Annie

Maryse Dawson

Published by Maryse Dawson, 2024.

This is a work of fiction. Similarities to real people, places, or events are entirely coincidental.

A PASSION FOR ANNIE

First edition. December 8, 2024.

ISBN: 979-8230871385

Written by Maryse Dawson.

Table of Contents

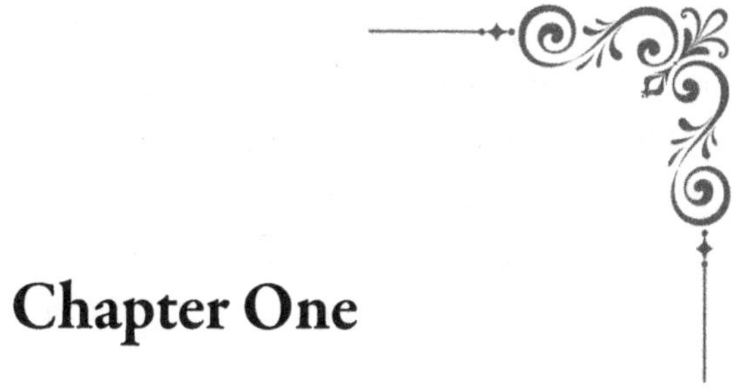

Chapter One

1879 Wyoming

The cold winter winds whipped across the Wyoming plains as Annie Johnson helped her father finish the evening chores on their small homestead. Though she was only twenty-three, she had taken on much of the responsibility of running the farm since her mother had passed the previous year. It had been hard, but she knew her mother would be just as proud of her as her father was. Together they had overcome grief and learned to carry on.

As she brushed down their lone milk cow, Beth, her thoughts drifted to the coming Christmas holiday. Money had been tight lately, and she wasn't sure what she could do to make the season easier for her father. She needed to do something to take both their minds off the memory of losing her mother.

It had been in the depths of winter that she had taken her last breath. She would never forget it. Even a year later, it was still a fresh memory.

Finishing up, she patted Beth on the neck and said softly. "You don't care, do you, girl? As long as you get your food, nothing really matters, does it?"

Beth eyed her sideways, her big tongue coming out to lick her lips and uttering a low moan before tucking back into the pile of hay.

"You see, you knew I was talking about food." Annie laughed. She turned around and threw the brush in an empty bucket, and slipping out of the pen, she closed the gate behind her. Beth was known to be a bit of an escape artist, and Annie had learned to take no chances.

Her father was fixing some fences in the far field, his figure just visible beyond the barn. He worked hard to keep their smallholding running efficiently, and she appreciated it. Unlike her friend Amy's father, who just sat around drinking and dishing out orders to her and her brother.

She pursed her lips. She disliked the man intensely. The best thing Amy could do was get married and leave home. But decent, law-abiding eligible men around these parts were scarce, so Amy just kept her head down and carried on.

Much like her own journey in life. She longed to find a husband, yet the thought of leaving her father weighed heavily on her heart. She knew he could never manage this place alone. Perhaps if she found a man willing to share their lives and help run the homestead, it could work. But for now, that remained a distant dream.

"Well, this won't do, Annie Johnson!" She tutted under her breath. "Dinner won't make itself."

She walked over to the water pump and began to draw some water into a bucket so she could wash her hands. Picking up the small bar of coarse soap, she rubbed it on her hands and wiped the day's grime away. The water was so cold that her hands began to turn red. Washing the suds off, she reached into her coat for a cloth and quickly dried them.

"Dang, it's so perishing cold." She grumbled, brushing her blonde hair off her face.

Just then, a rider came over the hill. She frowned, trying to make out who it was. They weren't expecting anyone, as far as she knew.

She waited patiently for the rider to approach near enough so she could identify them. It was a big horse, and the man astride it was equally as big. He was riding with ease, his long legs gripping the horse's flanks and urging it forwards towards her.

A few moments later, she recognised who it was—Jed Wheeler, the most prosperous farmer in the valley. But the look on his face said this wasn't a social call. He seemed very serious.

He was quite a bit older than her, mid-thirties or thereabouts, and on the few occasions their paths had crossed, she'd always found him a little intimidating. He was a handsome man, with shoulder-length dark-brown hair and piercing hazel eyes. He stood at least a foot taller than her and then some.

His eyes met hers as he reined in his horse. "Is your pa home?" he asked gruffly.

She nodded, apprehension building in her stomach. What did he want with her father? "He's in the far field, over there." She pointed her finger in the distance, and Jed turned his head to look. Without another word, he turned his horse and rode off to see him.

She watched him for a moment. Her gut felt uneasy. Something wasn't right. It wasn't just his tone but the look in his eyes. She nibbled on a fingernail, wondering whether she should go over and listen in but then decided against it. Dinner had to be done. They were having stew, and she just needed to add some more vegetables to finish it off. The meat had already been cooking for a couple of hours, so it should be tender by now.

Reluctantly, she drew her gaze away and headed towards the house.

Jed rode towards Abel Johnson with a determined mindset. He didn't like what he was going to say, but it had to be said.

He saw Abel's eyes flicker with concern as the noise of his horse alerted him to his presence. Jed dismounted, tilting his hat back, and walked over to him.

"Abel."

"Afternoon, Jed, what can I do for yuh?" Abel asked him cautiously. Jed could see in his eyes that he knew very well why he was there.

Jed cut straight to the point. "Your loan's six months overdue. I'm here to collect—one way or another."

"Has it been six months already?" Abel breathed, trying to stall. "I-I didn't realise it'd been so long, Jed. Truly, I didn't."

Jed quirked an eyebrow. "Abel, I sent you two letters; don't tell me you never received either of them."

"Well, I mean to say, I think I did receive one, but that was a while back and..."

"Do you have the means to pay me or not?" Jed asked, cutting to the chase. He wasn't a patient man at the best of times, and Abel's obvious attempt to forestall him was starting to grate.

"The harvest hasn't been good this year, Jed. Money's tight."

"So your answer is no." Jen said for him.

"Can yuh give me another six months? I promise yuh I'll do my best to get it for yuh"

"I've already given you six. I won't wait any longer."

Abel's eyes widened. "What're yuh gonna do? You're not gonna kill me, are yuh Jed?"

Jed shook his head. "I wouldn't do that, Abel. No, I'm going to take your daughter."

Abel took a step back in surprise. "What do yuh mean?"

"I need a woman to cook and clean around the place. The house is turning into a pigsty. From what I've seen of Annie, she's capable of just about anything, so I want her to become housekeeper for three months. In return, I'll cancel your debt."

Abel was quiet for a while. Jed remained silent, letting him mull over his offer. In all truth, Abel would be stupid to turn him down.

"And what if I don't agree? What if Annie doesn't agree?" Abel said warily.

"If you don't, I'll take enough of your horses to pay the debt. I've waited long enough. I'm not an unreasonable man, Abel; you know that. We all have our own debts and expenses. When I lent you that money for the seeds, you said you'd pay me back at the end of the harvest. You didn't."

Abel rubbed his forehead. "But what am I gonna do without my daughter to help around the place?"

"She can come back once a week to aid you. That's all. The rest of the time, she's mine."

"You ain't gonna hurt her, are yuh? 'Cause if yuh do, I'll hunt yuh down myself!" Abel said, his eyes narrowing with anger.

"I would never hurt her, Abel. You know me too well for that." He looked at him astutely. "So, do we have a deal?"

"I don't really have much choice, do I?"

"Not really, no."

"Very well, I'll have a word with her. If she agrees, that's fine, but if she doesn't, I'll find another way to pay yuh back. Somethin' that doesn't involve yuh takin' my horses." Abel said, reluctantly agreeing to his terms.

In three months' time, with a winter of hard work under Annie's belt, his debt would be paid. Jed remounted his horse and looked down at him. "I'll leave you to tell Annie, and I'll return in a week with the wagon. Make sure she's ready."

Annie heard the kitchen door open, just as she was taking the stew out of the oven. She placed the big pot on the table and turned around to look at her father. "What did Jed Wheeler want, Pa?"

Something about his expression made her stop dead still. "What is it, Pa? What's happened?"

"Come into the living room, Annie. There's somethin' I have to tell yuh."

She threw down her tea towel and followed him into the other room. He stopped in front of the fireplace and, placing one hand on the mantel, looked down into the flames.

"I've let yuh down, Annie."

Her heart almost stopped. What on earth had he done?

"I tried my best," he continued, "I really did, but I couldn't pay Jed the money I owed him."

Annie's eyes widened. She knew her father had borrowed money for seed after a bad harvest but hadn't realized how deep a hole they were in. She clasped her hands together nervously. "But I thought you'd paid him back?"

Her father shook his head sadly. "No, I should've told yuh before, but the time never seemed right."

"So what happens now?" Annie paced back and forth on the little rug. "Is he gonna take our house? Is that what he wants? We don't have anything else."

"He wants you."

Annie stopped pacing, and her jaw fell open. "Me?"

Her father nodded. "He wants yuh to work for him for three months, and then he'll cancel the debt."

Annie sat down on the nearest chair, her mind working fast. Jed wanted her to work for him. "What does he want me to do?"

"Cook and clean."

If it meant cancelling the debt, she could do that. Couldn't she? "But how will you cope on your own, Pa?"

"He said yuh can come back once a week to help out here. The rest of the time yuh have to be at his ranch."

She sat quietly for a moment in contemplation, nibbling on her fingernail. Jed was intimidating, and being in close proximity with him might prove to be a bit daunting. But their debt would be cancelled, and what was three months? She would be back in time to help with the next spring planting, and she could come back and help her father every week.

Besides which, she saw no other choice.

"I'm truly sorry, Annie." Her father said quietly. "And I understand if yuh don't want to go. I won't put any pressure on yuh. We can find some other way to pay him. He said he could take some of our horses."

Annie immediately leapt up and went over to hug him. "Pa, he ain't having our horses, that's for sure. Look, we can't raise that sort of money, so I don't want you to worry about it any more. I'll go to him. It's only for three months, and if it means our debt will be cancelled, then I can do it."

He patted her back. "You're a good daughter, Annie. Even when your pa lets yuh down."

"Oh, these things happen, Pa. Ain't for you to worry about now. I don't mind helping out, and three months will go by in the blink of an eye. Plus, I can come back every week to help you here." She kissed him on the cheek. "Come on, let's have dinner."

Although she said the words so confidently, it was mainly to appease her pa and put his mind at rest. Inside, she was quite daunted at the prospect of spending three months at Jed Wheeler's ranch. But as fate would have it, that's exactly what she was going to do.

A week later

Annie paced the living room, every now and then stopping to look out of the window. Jed was due today, and her bags were packed and ready to go.

Oh, Lord, she was so nervous!

Over the last week, she'd had a couple of occasions where she'd been close to backing out but the stakes were too high. The only alternative was giving Jed some of their thoroughbred horses, and that wasn't going to happen. Uh-uh.

No, she had to do this. Perhaps under Jed's stern exterior there was a soft heart? She pulled a face. He didn't look like he had a soft heart. Not at all.

A noise made her look up, and the man himself came into view, his wagon coming to a halt outside the front gate.

She closed her eyes for a moment to calm her nerves. Oh, Lord. She felt sick.

Swallowing hard, she straightened her back and walked over to the front door. Her father was already out the front talking to him. She stopped dead still for a moment to take a real good look at the man she would be living with for three months.

There was no denying that he cut a handsome figure. He was at least a head taller than her father, who was by no means a small man. But not only was Jed tall, but his shoulders were broad and strong, giving an overall appearance of strength.

He swivelled his head to look at her, his eyes locking with hers, and she felt colour fill her face at being caught in such blatant perusal.

Jed studied the petite little blonde that he'd come to collect. She was a pretty girl. Her curves were all in the right place, and her long blonde hair glistened in the winter sun. Her eyes were intelligent and a vibrant shade of blue.

But that wasn't why he wanted her at his ranch. He'd heard rumours of what a capable girl she was, and it was exactly what he needed.

His sister, Mary, had taken off four months ago. Run off with a travelling salesman of all things. He'd told her not to trust a man like that—he advised her until he was blue in the face—but it hadn't mattered a damn. She'd just left a note and gone.

He didn't have time for cleaning and the like. His ranch hands were the same. Food on the table had consisted of anything they could scrape together. None of them had a clue how to cook a decent meal.

As for cleaning and tidying, well, one look at his place, and Annie would most probably try and run back to her pa. But he was going to make sure that didn't happen. He needed her, and if she wanted her pa's debt cleared, then she'd have to tow the line.

He walked up to her, his eyes keenly assessing her flushed cheeks. "Afternoon, Annie. Your pa told me that you've agreed to come. I'm mighty glad you have."

"Oh?"

He nodded. "We need a woman's touch about the place." He didn't elaborate. He didn't want her to change her mind. Enough said. "Is this all your luggage?"

He looked down at the two carpet bags by her feet.

When she nodded, he picked them up and strode back to the wagon, calling gruffly over his shoulder, "Say your goodbyes; I want to get back before nightfall."

Lily trembled slightly at his tone. He was so intimidating, and it didn't seem to be a front; it just came naturally to him. Her father came to stand in front of her, his eyes sad. "If yuh want to back out, Annie, it won't bother me none."

She patted his arm, "No, Pa. I've made my mind up. Besides, I'll be back next week to visit. Don't you worry none about me."

She kissed him on the cheek and, taking a deep breath, headed over to the wagon. Jed was waiting for her, and before she could say a word, he placed his hands around her small waist and lifted her straight up onto the bench seat. Reaching for a blanket, he wrapped it over her lap and tucked it behind her.

The close proximity was a little disconcerting, and she risked a quick glance at his face. His eyes were a deep hazel framed by dark lashes. They were quite mesmerising and gulping; she realised she was unintentionally staring. Again.

Quickly, she looked down, but not before she heard a deep chuckle. Oh, so he found her amusing, did he? She bristled and pursed her lips. That was the second time he'd caught her staring.

As they set off across the darkening prairie, Annie looked around to see her pa standing out in front of the house. He looked so alone that she wanted to rush back and hug him. Closing her eyes for a moment to quell her emotions, she turned back to the horizon. She should learn to worry less, but it was hard. After all, he was all she had.

Their neighbour, Emiline Tompkins, or Emmy to her friends, was going to call in every now and then to see how her pa was faring. She was a widow, and Annie secretly thought she was sweet on her pa. Not that he noticed. But just knowing she would be there for him made Annie's current task a lot easier.

As they rode, Annie stole glances at Jed as he sat beside her, his workroughened hands gripping the reins with ease. Though his reputation preceded him as a stern, no-nonsense man, she couldn't help but admire his profile. There weren't many men that handsome in her neck of the woods.

They soon arrived at Jed's large ranch house. "You'll have your chores outlined tomorrow," he said gruffly as he helped her down off the wagon, again putting his hands around her waist and lifting her onto the ground as though she weighed no more than a feather.

He picked up her bags and then led her up the wooden steps into the house. It was dark inside, and apart from the fire with its embers burning low, she couldn't make out much.

Lighting a candle, Jed swiftly showed her up the stairs and into a small bedroom. "I'll leave you to get settled in. Come down when you're ready in the morning, and I'll introduce you to everyone." He left the candle with her, and the next minute, he was gone.

Annie stood for a moment and looked around the room. In the candlelight, it looked quite cosy. The bed was made, and there was a pitcher of water on a small table in one corner. But it was cold. Damn cold.

Opening one of her carpet bags, she drew out some clothes and laid them on the bed, sifting through them until she found her night attire. With lightning speed, she undressed, throwing on her nightdress and quickly placed a shawl around her shoulders for extra warmth. She was going to need it!

Climbing beneath the covers, she snuggled down and curled into a ball, trying to keep her body warm. Too exhausted to ponder what lay ahead, Annie quickly blew out the candle and fell into a deep sleep.

Chapter Two

The next morning, Annie awoke early. Stretching in bed, she opened her eyes and blinked slowly as her mind registered where she was—Jed's ranch.

She sat up and shivered as the bed covers slipped down, exposing her lightly clad body to the chill air. That was something she was going to have to do—make sure a fire was lit in her room. She hated feeling the cold. She listened to see if there was any noise coming from downstairs, but the house seemed quiet.

Sliding her legs from the bed, she quickly dressed, choosing a practical day dress in colours of beige and brown. Brushing her hair, she plaited it into one long braid. When her hair was out of the way, she found cleaning tasks a lot easier. A quick wash, and she was ready to face the day.

She made her way down the wooden stairs, eager to see the ranch and her new home for the next few months.

The curtains were still drawn and made everything appear gloomy. Starting in the living room, she pulled the curtains back and quickly shielded her face when clouds of dust flew up into the air, making her sneeze.

She flapped her hand around to disperse the particles, her face screwing up. "Goodness me!" She breathed, trying not to cough.

As daylight flooded the rooms, Annie's eyes widened at the state of disarray. The kitchen counters were piled high with dirty dishes, a thick layer of dust covered the furniture, and muddy boot prints tracked across the living room floor. There were even cobwebs hanging from the wooden beams. "Lord! No wonder Jed needs my help!" she muttered to herself.

Just then, the man himself came stomping in from outside, snow dusting his shoulders. The room seemed to shrink as his large form seemed to take up so much space.

"Morning," he grunted, looking at her a little warily. "Sleep alright?"

"Yes, thank you," Annie replied, then gestured around the room. "What the hell happened here? Did a herd of cattle run through it?"

Jed's stern visage changed a bit, and he let out a low chuckle. "You haven't met the ranch hands yet, have you? They're a little uncivilised."

He walked over to the kitchen range and stoked the fire before turning back to face her. "That's why you're here. This place needs tidying." He reached into a cupboard and pulled out an apron. "You'd better get this on—the hands'll be coming in for breakfast soon enough."

Annie's jaw dropped. "How in tarnation am I meant to prepare a meal? I have to tidy before I do anything!" She protested.

He gave her a low smile. "Well, you'd better get to it then."

"But...!"

And he was gone, the door banging closed behind him. For a moment, Annie just stood there, feeling close to tears. Everything was such a mess! In fact, she'd never seen such disarray.

Closing her eyes for a moment, she squared her shoulders and took a deep breath. She could do this. Her father's debt depended on it. Pushing her sleeves up to her elbows, she tied the apron around her waist and began to get stuck in.

Half an hour later, Jed returned, this time accompanied by a group of rugged cowboys. When he entered the house, he was surprised to see a difference already. For a start, he could actually see the floor.

His ranch hands began stomping snow off their heavy leather boots.

"Mornin' Miss Annie!" Billy tipped his hat at her. "Did yuh sleep well?"

Jed had already told them that Annie was here and that they were to be on their best behaviour and especially to mind their manners.

Annie gave a polite smile, then cleared her throat. "Gentlemen, if you don't mind removing your boots before coming inside? I've just finished sweeping, and I'd rather not have to do it all over again."

Jed quirked an eyebrow and watched his men exchange amused glances, but they reluctantly complied. "Yes'm," Billy said with a twinkle in his eye. "Wouldn't want to ruin your hard work."

Luke sniffed the air as he almost overbalanced ripping his boots off. "Somethin' sure smells nice!"

Jack digged him in the ribs. "That's for me! You ain't gettin' none!"

Danny was already pulling a chair out and taking a seat. "I'm the first seated, so I'm the first gettin' served! Right?" He sat at the table, looking smug. But it didn't last long.

Marvin cuffed him around the head as he took a seat next to him. He was older by a few years. "Respect yer elders! I'm before you."

Jed watched the exchange with a hint of a smile and stroked a hand over his beard, wondering how Annie was going to deal with them all. She turned her back on them and stirred a pot of something. He wasn't sure what, but he agreed with his men; it sure smelled good.

As she bustled about, her determination and no-nonsense attitude was already making an impression. It proved to him that he'd made the right decision. Most women he knew would have run for the hills after taking a look at the ranch.

She turned around and placed several plates on the table, then some mugs, and then finally a big pot of coffee. "Help yourselves to coffee whilst I finish breakfast."

There was a big scramble to see who got hold of the pot first; Luke won, and with a look of triumph, he poured his coffee first. The others impatiently waited their turn. When Luke went to pass it along, Jed coughed loudly, and Luke immediately passed it to him. No one messed with Jed.

Jed sat back in his seat, sipping his coffee, which he had to say was a damned sight finer than his own brew, whilst he waited for breakfast to be served.

It didn't take long. Annie placed a big plate of cornbread in the centre of the table and then a big pan of scrambled eggs, another of fried potatoes, and a big plate of bacon. "I'll just get the hot cakes."

She turned her back, and the next minute all of the ranch hands steamed in like they hadn't eaten in days. Bread flew across the table; the scrambled eggs ended up half on their plates, half on the table. It was a complete mess

Suddenly, there was a loud banging as Annie bashed a ladle against a copper pan. "What in tarnation are you doing?" She yelled. "Stop this at once!"

His ranch hands stopped in surprise, their faces all turning to hers. She put the pot and ladle down and admonished them. "Don't any of you say grace before you eat? Have you no manners?"

There was a lot of shuffling and muttering. Jed hid a smile and looked down at the table. She was something when she was angry!

She took a seat next to him, and eyeing the others with determination, she clasped her hands together and closed her eyes. She said a brief prayer and then looked at them and said, "Now you may eat."

Again, bedlam broke out as they reached for the food. Jed looked directly at Annie and shrugged.

Annie tutted under her breath. She had never seen such behaviour. They were like wild men. Reaching for a piece of cornbread, she placed it on Jed's plate. "I don't think you're going to see any of the scrambled eggs, do you?"

He shook his head. His eyes were glinting with mirth, and she couldn't help but smile back. He looked even more handsome when he smiled. Perhaps he would do it more often now that she was here?

She looked down the table, watching the flurry of arms and hands as the ranch hands devoured in minutes what it had taken her a good while to make. Lord, did she have a lot of work on her hands in more ways than one? She watched them stuff the food down their necks like men possessed and shook her head.

Only a few moments later, the food was gone, and Marvin let out a loud belch. Annie gasped and shot him a look of outrage. "If you want to continue eating at this table, then you will refrain from doing that again."

Marvin had the grace to look a little sheepish. "Pardon, Annie. I'll try to remember."

Danny laughed loudly, and Marvin shot him a look of annoyance, clenching his fist at him. Danny quickly looked away, whistling nonchalantly, looking like butter wouldn't melt.

Jed swigged the rest of his coffee down and stood up. "Come on, back to work. The livestock ain't gonna look after themselves!" He gave a curt nod to Annie, and shrugging on their coats and boots, the men soon left the house.

Annie sat there quietly for a moment, looking at the dishes and plates on the table, mixed with spilled remnants of food. For a brief moment, she felt like packing her bags and fleeing back home, but that wasn't her. She had more backbone than that.

She'd accepted this challenge, and she would see it through. By hook or by crook!

Standing up, she set to work with determined efficiency. She cleared the table, washed everything up, scrubbed the countertops until they shone, swept the floors free of dirt and debris, and even managed to dust the mantel and bookshelves.

Two hours later, she stopped to survey her work. The ranch looked so much cleaner and tidier. The same couldn't be said for her. She could feel the stray bits of hair poking out of her plait, and her face was surely covered in a layer of grime from all the dust.

Throwing off her apron, she rushed upstairs and had a quick wash and brush up before heading back to the kitchen to begin the preparations for lunch.

By the time the ranch hands returned for the midday meal, the once-dishevelled living room had been transformed. Annie had just finished setting the table when the men trudged in, removing their boots at the door as she had instructed earlier. She was happy to note that they did as she had previously asked without having to ask again.

"Smells mighty fine in here, Annie," Danny commented. The others murmured in agreement as they took their seats. She smiled as she turned her back to start serving up the meal. It was quite satisfying to have them appreciate her cooking. Her pa always had, but she was never sure if that was just him being polite.

Lifting the big pot, she placed it in the centre of the table and took off the lid. Each of them sniffed the air, their eyes widening.

"Well, damn, if that don't smell like the best thing, this side of the Mississippi!" Jack exclaimed.

Annie took their plates one by one and served them all a generous helping of the meat stew. She then placed a big plate of bread on the table.

Before digging in, Jed bowed his head. "Let's give thanks," he rumbled. The others followed suit, as Jed offered a brief prayer for the meal and the hard work ahead.

Annie was amazed that things could be turned around so suddenly. Maybe Jed had had a word with them behind her back. But either way, she was delighted with the change.

Once they began eating the hearty stew Annie had prepared, the men made a concerted effort to mind their manners. There was little idle chatter, save for the occasional compliment on the delicious food. Annie felt a sense of satisfaction watching them enjoy the fruits of her labour.

As Jed took a sip of freshly ground coffee, he met Annie's gaze across the table. "You've done good work here, Annie," he said gruffly. "The place is spotless."

Annie felt a flush of pride. "Thank you, Jed. I aim to keep it that way. Talking of which, I'd like to go into town and buy some new fabric so I can make some curtains."

"We don't need 'em." He said, shaking his head.

"Well, of course you need them." She eyed the torn excuse for curtains that were hanging haphazardly from the rails. "You can't keep those ones!"

"We don't need 'em." He repeated, standing up.

"You might not need them as such, but you could certainly do with them." She argued. "If I could just get one of the boys to give me a ride to town, I can..."

He raised his hand. "I said, no."

"But..."

"Don't argue with me, Annie." He eyed her sternly, shrugging on his coat and boots.

With one last look, he turned around and left the kitchen, the door banging behind him. Danny glanced at her and said, "He's not one for fripperies and such, Annie. Best forget the idea."

When the men had left, Annie sat there, tapping her fingernails on the table. She wouldn't forget it at all. New curtains would bring the place alive with some colour which it badly needed. The place was lacking a woman's touch, and as she was the only woman, then it was down to her to put things right. He was a man—what did he know?

She narrowed her eyes, deep in thought. She'd bet he had a tab in town. He must have. She'd just buy some pretty fabric, needles, and thread and simply put them on his tab. By the time he found out, the curtains would be up and hanging, looking beautiful, and there wouldn't be a dang thing he could do about it! She sniggered to herself. That would teach him for being so brusque!

When Annie had finished tidying the mess from lunch, she put on her warm winter coat, pulled on her boots, and headed outside to find Jed.

He was standing, watching Billy trying to break in one of their horses. He looked down at her as she approached his side, and she eyed him confidently. "Is anyone going into town this week?"

"Why?" His tone was gruff as usual and tinged with suspicion.

She raised her small chin. "Oh, I just wanted to buy a few extra items of food for the larder. Do you have a tab?"

He crossed his arms over his chest and narrowed his eyes a little. "I do. I have one with all the shops in town. They know me to be a man of integrity. I always pay my bills."

"Oh, well, then that's perfect. I can just put it on your tab. The food, I mean."

"Uh-huh." He ran a hand over his beard and added, "Don't think of buying anything else but the food, do you hear?"

"Of course, I won't!" She said, her eyes wide and as innocent as she could make them. "So who's going into town and when?"

"Jack's taking the wagon in a couple of days."

"Perfect!" She shot him a happy smile and turned to go back to the house, but he caught her by the elbow, stopping her in her tracks.

"Whilst you're here, I'll show you around the ranch. You haven't had a chance to see it properly yet."

"No, I haven't." She replied, looking up at him. "I'd like that."

He called over to Billy, telling him he was going to show her around and then holding out his arm for her to take, she placed her small hand on his sleeve, and they set off towards the barns.

He had quite a few cattle inside the big barn; the rest were out in the fields grazing; the thin layer of snow was no problem for their searching tongues. They were pretty much acclimatized, so the cold didn't bother them much.

Another barn held some horses, and in one corner, lots of chickens. Although they weren't penned in, they could come and go as they pleased.

"We also plant wheat and corn." He said proudly.

Suddenly, out of nowhere, a cat went whizzing by her feet, followed quickly by one of the dogs, barking and growling in its haste to catch the cat. The dog knocked against her legs, unbalancing her, and she fell straight against Jed, clutching onto him for dear life.

He held her steady, an amused look in his eyes. "You've gotta watch out for those two. Milly, the cat, is always antagonising Fred. I should've warned you earlier."

The barking faded into the distance as the pair disappeared outside and Annie realised she was still holding onto Jed. Embarrassed, she quickly pulled herself away, her cheeks flushing beet red.

"Oh, dear me." She muttered. "They gave me a bit of a fright."

"They're rascals, the pair of them. At least you know to look out for them now." He grinned, and for a moment, Annie was mesmerised. What a difference a smile could make. She felt a sudden ripple of desire shoot through her, and flustered, she said quickly, "Well, I'd better get back to prepare dinner." She started to walk away and then added, "Thank you for showing me around."

"My pleasure." He drawled.

She quickly left the barn and headed indoors. Her cheeks were still flushed, and she just couldn't forget how large his muscles had felt beneath her fingertips when she'd fallen against him. He smelled good too. Woodsmoke and leather.

Shaking her head, she pursed her lips and said aloud, "Annie Johnson, quit daydreaming and get indoors!"

She headed inside, and taking off her boots and coat, she set about preparing the evening meal.

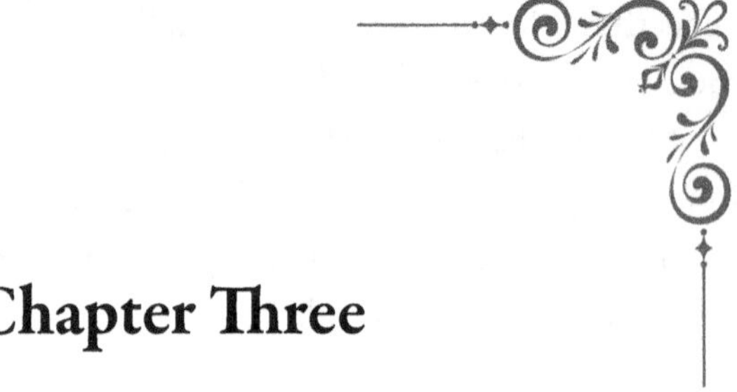

Chapter Three

Two days later

After breakfast, Annie climbed aboard the wagon with Jack, one of the ranch hands, as they prepared to head into the small town nearby.

She was quite excited to visit the store, and there was nothing quite like getting out in the fresh air, even if it was dang cold.

"Take this, Annie," Jack said, handing her a blanket. "It'll keep you warm for the trip."

"Oh, thank you, Jack," Annie replied with a smile, laying it straight over her lap. "I appreciate you taking me with you to town today."

"Ain't nothin'," Jack assured her. "Jed wants me to pick up a few supplies, and I'm happy to let you tag along." He grinned, winking at her.

Jed stood on the porch, watching them from a distance. His large figure leaning nonchalantly against one of the posts, his expression brooding. Annie waved at him as Jack flicked the reins, and with a little nod, he turned his back and went inside.

The ride along the way was bumpy but peaceful, the crisp winter air invigorating. She was thankful Jack had given her the blanket, though, because one thing she hated was being cold. Her bonnet, tied with a pretty red ribbon under her chin, kept her head warm, and she had her hand muffler to keep her hands from turning into lumps of ice.

"Have you worked for Jed for very long?" She asked Jack.

"Couple of years now. I enjoy the work, and he's a fair man to work for. Couldn't ask for better. His sister was a tad irksome, and to be honest with you, Annie, you cook a whole lot better than she ever did."

"Oh, that's nice of you to say." Annie said, feeling genuinely pleased. "I didn't know Jed had a sister."

Jack shook his head. "He don't talk about her much. Ever since she eloped with Evan."

"Oh?"

"Evan's a salesman. He came by a few times a year to sell his wares. Mostly rubbish. But Mary fell for his charms, and even though Jed warned her off him, she dang well ran off with the bast... I mean, the scoundrel." He frowned. "To be honest, I think Jed would pulverise him if he set eyes on him again."

"Oh, lord!" Annie exclaimed, picturing the scenario in her head. "So, I guess Mary used to do the cooking and cleaning?"

"Yes, ma'am. But her food wasn't as nice, and she didn't make things look as pretty as you do." He cleared his throat. "I mean, around the house, you know..."

"Oh, sure, I know what you mean, Jack."

She sat quietly contemplating his words whilst the wagon rumbled its way along the track. Jed had never mentioned Mary, but perhaps he was ashamed of her. She might ask him about her, given the opportune moment.

They arrived in town, and Jack positioned the wagon out of the front of a big mercantile store. He graciously helped her down onto the ground.

As they entered the general store, the bell above the door jingled to announce their arrival. Jack immediately made a beeline for the counter, where the shopkeeper greeted him by name.

"Mornin' Jack! The usual?" the shopkeeper asked.

"Yes, sir," Jack nodded before turning to Annie. "I'm just gonna grab some chewin' tobacco. Why don't you look around and get what you need?"

"Thank you," Annie said, already scanning the shelves. She picked up a few bars of lye soap, some ground coffee and then hesitantly made her way to the fabric section. Glancing around to make sure Jack was occupied, she quickly selected a bolt of soft cotton and some sewing needles, discreetly tucking them into a separate bag that the shopkeeper's wife gave to her. "It's a surprise, so I don't want Jack to see," she explained, smiling sweetly.

"Oh, of course, ma'am. I'll put it on Mr. Wheeler's tab when you've gone." She tapped her nose.

"Find everything alright, miss?" the shopkeeper inquired as Annie approached the counter.

"Yes, thank you. Your wife just helped me get these." Annie replied, trying to keep her voice casual. She didn't want Jack to know about the sewing supplies. She'd bought a bit more than she needed to make some simple curtains and was hoping she had enough left over to maybe even make a quilt or two to brighten up the ranch house.

As the shopkeeper tallied up her purchases, Annie kept a watchful eye on Jack, hoping he wouldn't notice her extra bag.

Thankfully, Jack seemed engrossed in his conversation with the shopkeeper, discussing the latest ranch gossip. Annie breathed a quiet sigh of relief as they exited the store, ready to head back to the ranch.

Jed watched the wagon roll past as he strode towards the house. Annie's cheeks were flushed from the cold, and he couldn't help but notice that she looked as pretty as a picture. Her blonde hair was glinting in the sunlight, and her expression was uplifting, to say the least. Something that had been missing from his life for a while.

His thoughts turned to his sister. Mary was a rebellious little madam, but her vibrant personality always perked everyone up. Having Annie in the house filled that gap and then some.

When she'd fallen against him yesterday, it had taken all his willpower not to throw her back in his arms and kiss the hell out of her. Her soft little body enveloped in his embrace had made him realise what he was missing in his life: a woman.

She was a lot younger than he was, and he doubted she'd want a big, rugged, uncouth man like him for a husband. But there wasn't anything wrong with yearning for something you couldn't have.

Striding over to the wagon, he reached up and put his hands around Annie's tiny waist, lifting her down onto the ground with ease.

"Did you get everything you wanted?" He asked.

"Oh, yes. The shopkeepers were most helpful."

"Sam and Megan McGill have owned the store for years now. Always helpful and always happy." He reached for her bag. "Do you need help with that?"

"Oh, thank you, no." She replied quickly, "But the box in the back of the wagon is heavy."

He walked around and picked up a couple of the boxes with ease, following her as she led the way inside the house, her trim little figure bustling along quickly, almost too quickly. He frowned. Was she hiding something, or was it just him? He was an astute man, and something was telling him that something wasn't right.

Placing the two boxes on the table, he stepped aside as Jack entered with some more. "That's all of it." Jack said.

"Thanks, Jack." Jed replied, "Billy could do with some help in the cowshed."

"Sure, Jed." He disappeared back out of the door, and Annie walked over to it, taking her boots off and placing them neatly to one side.

"I'll just take my bag up to my room." She said, "Shall I make some coffee in a minute?"

He nodded and took a seat at the table, listening to her light feet as she went up the staircase. He tapped his fingers on the table whilst waiting, wondering if he should say anything but then decided against it. Whatever it was, it would come out in the wash sooner or later.

Standing up, he opened the boxes and began to pull out the food and goods, laying them out on the table. It felt good to not have to do it on his own for a change. Having a woman about the place made his life a lot easier. It might only be for three months, but he appreciated it.

After secretly stashing her bag of sewing supplies under the bed, Annie made her way downstairs to the kitchen, ready to make a fresh brew of coffee. She was surprised to find Jed had already unpacked the boxes of supplies they'd picked up in town.

"Jed, you didn't have to do all this," Annie said gratefully as she began brewing a fresh pot of coffee.

"Wasn't no trouble," Jed grunted, as gruff as ever, taking a seat at the table. "Figured I'd get it sorted while you were upstairs."

Annie poured him a steaming mug of coffee and then joined him at the table. She paused momentarily, gathering her courage. "I, um, heard a bit of talk from Jack about your sister. Is everything alright?"

Jed let out a heavy sigh, his handsome features etched with concern. "Well, about as alright as they can be, I reckon. Mary, up and eloped with a slick-talking salesman. Ran off and just left me a note."

Annie's eyes widened. "Jack said as much. That must have been so difficult for you. I can only imagine how worried you must be."

"That's just it—I ain't worried, not really," Jed admitted. "My sister's always been a headstrong girl. Guess I shouldn't be surprised she'd pull a stunt like this." He shook his head ruefully. "Still, it doesn't make it any easier."

"I see," Annie murmured sympathetically. "Did you try to find her?"

Jed met her gaze and shrugged, "I tried, but they were long gone by the time I read that letter. I just hope she's happy, but something tells me she'll regret it."

"Would you have her back again?" Annie said.

"Yes, I wouldn't turn her away, but I would give her a hell of a belting."

Annie almost stopped breathing. "A what?"

"A belting. I'm the head of the household now that Pa's passed away, and I would be the one to punish her." He tilted his head. "Doesn't your pa punish you when you're bad?"

Annie shook her head, feeling a little faint. "Nope. I ain't ever had the belt taken to me."

"You seem quite headstrong. I'm surprised you ain't received a whipping ever."

Annie gulped. Good lord. She chewed her bottom lip with worry. This put a whole new prospect on her actions today. What if he found out? Would he take a belt to her? She felt a frisson of alarm ripple through her but also a jolt of excitement. What the heck made her feel excited about that?!

She realised Jed was watching her intently. "Are you alright?"

She nodded, her mouth suddenly as dry as dust. They sat in contemplative silence for a moment, sipping their coffee.

"Well, enough of my troubles," Jed finally declared, straightening in his chair. "What else did you get in town? Anything I should know about?"

Annie felt herself flush, remembering the sewing supplies hidden upstairs. "Oh, no, I just bought myself a couple of new hankies; nothing too exciting," she replied airily. "I'll get started on putting these supplies away."

Jed eyed her curiously as she stood up, but thankfully he didn't press the matter further.

“I’ll go and help Billy and Jack.” He said, scraping his chair back and getting to his feet, “I’ll be back for lunch.”

When he’d left, Annie placed a hand over her chest and said aloud, “What have I gone and done?”

That evening, as the ranch hands retired to their quarters at the back of the house, Annie stayed up late by the soft glow of a single candle. She carefully unfolded the bolt of cotton fabric she’d purchased in town, her fingers tracing the delicate pattern. It was so pretty and would make the kitchen look cosy and inviting.

Part of her was hesitant to even begin sewing—what if Jed discovered her secret project and asked her where she got the money? But another part of her was determined to brighten up the drab ranch house and make it feel more like a home. Perhaps if she just hung the curtains discreetly, no one would be the wiser. Most men didn’t really notice things like furnishings.

With a resolute nod, Annie set to work, meticulously measuring and cutting the fabric. She lost herself in the rhythmic motion of the needle and thread, her brow furrowing in concentration. Before long, she had fashioned a pair of simple yet charming curtains.

The next morning, she arose early and carefully hung the new curtains in the kitchen, stepping back to admire her handiwork. Just as she was smoothing out a stray wrinkle, a voice startled her.

"Mornin', Annie. Those are some mighty fine curtains."

Annie whirled around to see Luke, one of the ranch hands, standing in the doorway. "Oh! Good morning, Luke. I, um, I hope you don't mind. I just thought the room could use a bit of brightening up."

Luke chuckled, his eyes twinkling. "Not at all, ma'am. Adds a nice touch, if you ask me." He tipped his hat and settled himself at the table.

Annie let out a breath she didn't realize she'd been holding and quickly went to his side. "Can you not mention the curtains to anyone, please?"

He looked puzzled. "Well, yeah, I guess, if you don't want me saying nothin'."

Annie nodded her head vigorously. "I'd rather you didn't."

So far, so good. Perhaps Jed wouldn't even notice the new curtains.

Half-way through breakfast, Annie began to relax. No one had mentioned anything. They all happily tucked into the food she'd prepared for them, and not a word was said. She sipped on her coffee and smiled to herself. Perfect. She knew she'd been right when she thought men wouldn't notice. I mean, the only reason Luke had noticed was because she'd been fiddling with the damn things!

But as they filed out after the meal, Jed remained seated at the table, his gaze fixed on Annie as she leaned against the counter.

"Alright, Annie, spill the beans," Jed said gruffly. "Where'd you get the money for those curtains?"

Annie felt her heart drop. Oh, Lord. How was she going to get out of this one? She opted on side-tracking him. "I, um, I just wanted to make the place a little more cheerful, that's all."

Jed leaned back in his chair, his brow furrowed. "Now, I know full well you ain't got no money of your own. So where'd you get it?"

Seeing no other choice, Annie took a deep breath and said in a rush. "I put it on your tab at the mercantile store yesterday. I know I should've asked your permission first, but...

"The hell you did!" Jed interrupted, his voice rising. "That money was for necessities, not frivolous decorations."

Annie shrunk back, her hands trembling. "I'm sorry, Jed. I just thought..."

"Thought what?" Jed cut her off again, his face etched with displeasure. "What did I say to you yesterday?"

"Errr...!"

"When you asked me, I said no. Do you remember?"

She nodded, looking down at the ground. This wasn't good.

She heard the chair scrape back, and then he was right in front of her. She gulped and looked up at him.

"Do you know what happens when someone disobeys me, Annie?"

She shook her head, her eyes wide.

"They get punished. And you, my girl, are going to get a sound spanking for that little prank."

"But Jed!" She began to back away, but he put his hand around her wrist and pulled her into the living room. She tried to dig her heels into the floor, but he was too big to argue with.

"Please, Jed? This ain't fair!"

He stopped for a moment and looked down at her, his expression stern. "Did you or did you not go behind my back?"

She winced. "Well, when you put it like that..."

"Exactly. It was dishonest behaviour and I won't tolerate it. In this house, if you misbehave, you get punished, so now you're going to get a good hiding."

"No!" She tried to pull back, but as he took a seat, she soon found herself thrown over his lap, her feet off the floor and her hands scrabbling against the floorboards. "You can't do this!"

"I can do whatever I want, little girl. This is my house, my rules."

He laid his hand on her back, holding her down, and added, "Unless, of course, you want to go back home, but then your father's debt will still have to be paid. So it's your choice. What's it to be?"

Annie closed her eyes. "I guess I don't have any choice, do I?" She spat, her anger coming to the fore. "Just so you know, I hate you."

"I'm sure you do, you little madam, but you have to learn that when I say something, I mean it."

Annie rolled her eyes and resigned herself to her fate. She should never have gone against such a man as Jed.

Chapter Four

Jed looked down at the sassy, defiant little baggage laying over his lap and shook his head. Reaching for the hem of her dress, he drew it straight over her back and then parted her bloomers, revealing her peachy little bottom to his appreciative gaze. It was perfect.

Focussing his mind on the task at hand, he swiftly brought his hand swinging down onto both buttocks, the resounding slap echoing around the room, shortly followed by her shocked gasp.

"*Oh!*"

He quickly set up a steady rhythm of sharp, stinging smacks onto her delectable little bottom, watching the alabaster skin change to a beautiful rosy pink.

She tried her best to stop him, kicking her legs and wailing, but it didn't make a jot of difference. She'd behaved badly, and he wasn't one for putting up with folk thinking they could act how they liked. Not in his house, and it didn't matter who they were.

He paused for a moment, admiring his handiwork and feeling the heat from her sizzling bottom beneath his palm.

"I reckon you owe me an apology, little girl."

He thought he heard a cuss and leaned in nearer. "What was that?"

"I'm sorry." Judging by her tone, her pride was smarting just as much as her backside. Smiling to himself, he gave her one last big smack, straight across both cheeks, and then released his hold on her.

She jumped up like a scalded cat, her eyes blazing fire at him as she hopped from one foot to the other, clutching her bottom.

"I'm not gonna be able to sit down properly now!" She huffed, her brows knitting together as she met his gaze.

He raised an eyebrow. "And whose fault is that?"

Her eyes darkened and her bottom lip pouted with self-pity, but she refrained from any further backchat. She knew she was in the wrong. Simple as.

He stood up and walked over to her, placing his hand on her chin and forcing her to look at him. "I hope you've learned your lesson."

She nodded and lowered her lashes.

"Good. I'm going out to help the boys. I'll see you at lunch."

After Jed's stern reprimand, Annie retreated to her room, needing a moment to gather her thoughts. She lay down on her front on the bed, her hands trembling slightly. She hadn't anticipated Jed reacting so harshly to her small act of decorating.

"I was just trying to make this place a little more like home," she murmured to herself, smoothing the quilt beneath her fingers.

Her bottom was still throbbing. He had such enormous hands. Good Lord. One thing was certain: she wouldn't be sitting down for dinner and dang what any of the ranch hands thought. She certainly wasn't going to explain that their boss had just spanked her like a naughty child.

She closed her eyes for a moment, mortified.

Resolving to be more mindful of Jed's rules in the future, Annie took a deep breath, wriggled off the bed, and headed back downstairs. As she prepared the lunchtime meal—a hearty stew and freshly baked bread—the ranch hands trickled in one by one. To her delight, they all dutifully removed their boots and took their seats around the table. It seemed they were finally getting house trained.

When Jed entered, Annie nervously waited for him to comment on the curtains again. But to her surprise, he simply nodded in her direction and took a seat at the table like nothing had happened. She breathed a sigh of relief, and whilst the men were talking amongst themselves, she placed the big pot of stew in the middle of the table and a plate of fresh bread either side so they could help themselves.

She stood to say grace, and Billy frowned at her. “Ain’t you gonna sit down, Miss Annie?”

“I’d rather not; thank you all the same.”

She darted a glance at Jed to find him staring back at her, his expression unreadable. Well, she had no clue what he was thinking, but at least he wasn’t laughing at her, and he also hadn’t revealed to the others what had happened. That was something.

Billy didn’t press the matter. She didn’t give him the chance. She just quickly said grace and told them to help themselves to the bread whilst she dished out the stew.

Soon enough, their plates were filled, and the oddity of her standing up seemed to disappear as they found other topics to talk about.

As they ate, she was heartened to hear Jack compliment the fresh, clean scent of his freshly laundered clothes.

"Much obliged, Annie," he said with a grateful smile. "Ain't nothing better than putting on a crisp, clean shirt."

Annie beamed, feeling a sense of satisfaction in her work. Perhaps she was making more of an impression than she realized. Her mind immediately went to the curtains, and she dismissed them from her mind. That was an error that perhaps she wouldn't make in the future!

During the afternoon, she busied herself with dusting and cleaning the living area. The hearth needed a good seeing to; the darned thing hadn’t been cleaned properly in ages. She ended up getting more soot on herself than anything. But in the end, everything looked nice and bright. She stood back and surveyed her handiwork.

“Done a good job there, girl.” A gruff voice said behind her. She turned around to find Jed standing in the doorway, his arms folded and nodding his head as he looked around the room. He settled his eyes on her and, with a faint smile on his face, walked over to her. "I think you need to go and clean up." He raised a hand and wiped a bit of soot off her face. It was an intimate moment, and Annie suddenly found her heart beating faster than it should and her breath a little shallower than usual.

Up close, she could see the flecks of colours in his hazel eyes and found she couldn't look away. He stared back at her, not saying a word, his eyes locked with hers.

It was only the sound of the door opening that made them both move away from one another.

It was Luke. "Hey, Jed, you ain't seen Billy, have yuh? I asked him to help me with cleaning out the stables, and I ain't seen hide nor hair of him since!"

Jed sighed. "It's not one of his favourite jobs, is it? Come on, I'll help you. We'll sort Billy out when we find him."

He winked at Annie, and the two men left the house. Annie stood there for a moment, feeling a little perplexed. Jed had actually winked at her. Was the big man thawing a little?

Later that evening, as the ranch hands retired to the bunkhouse, Annie settled gingerly into a rocking chair by the fire with a well-worn book—a very clean rocking chair, she might say, thanks to her. She shifted a little to get more comfortable because her bottom was still tender from Jed's great big mitts. Opening the book, she began to read.

She was so engrossed in the story that she didn't notice Jed enter the room until he cleared his throat.

"Evening, Annie," he said gruffly, taking a seat across from her. "What're you reading'?"

Annie glanced up, a flush creeping up her cheeks. "Oh, just an old favourite of mine—*Pride and Prejudice*," she replied. "It's a lovely story."

Jed quirked an eyebrow, "Is that so? How about you read me a bit of it, then?"

Annie blinked in surprise but quickly recovered. "Of course." She began reading aloud, her voice soft and melodic as she described the world of the Bennet sisters and their charming suitors. Albeit one a bit stern like someone sitting right next to her!

As she read, she glanced at Jed out of the corner of her eye to see if he was actually listening or just humouring her. But he was indeed listening, his big frame leaning back in his chair and his gaze fixed intently on her. Annie felt a curious fluttering in her chest, suddenly very aware of his presence.

When she reached the end of the chapter, Jed nodded approvingly. "That was real nice," he murmured. "You've got a way with words. Reckon I could get used to hearing more of that."

Annie smiled shyly. "I'd be happy to read to you again, Jed. Whenever you'd like." and she was sincere about that. It had been nice sharing a quiet moment with him.

Jed's lips curved upward in a faint smile of his own. "I'll hold you to that, little girl."

With that, he stood up and said goodnight, the deep timbre of his voice making her breathing shallow again. Good lord, what was wrong with her?

She watched him go as he headed off to his own bedroom; he was so tall and broad that he had to lower his head a little to take the stairs.

She closed her book shut and laid her head back on the chair. Perhaps, despite their rocky start, she and Jed were finding a way to understand each other after all. The fact that he liked her book was a good beginning.

Was Jed someone she could consider spending her life with, though? I mean, he spanked her bottom for goodness sake. Would she want a husband that held her accountable like that?

She chewed her bottom lip, thinking hard, and decided that she'd just wait and see how things progressed. She could be jumping the gun. Just because she felt a stirring; didn't mean to say he felt the same. In fact, he most probably wouldn't want a wife that was so disobedient, not after the way he'd spanked her backside.

But there was something about going over his lap that she'd found exciting. She had no idea why. Surely she should feel the exact opposite.

Sighing, she stood up and decided to go to bed herself. Her mind was awhirl with too many thoughts, and she needed to get some rest. She was off home tomorrow to see her pa, and she wanted to be refreshed.

Humming to herself, she made her way upstairs and tried to push all thoughts of the massive Jed out of her mind, which was fine, until she put her head on the pillow and the only thing she could think about was him.

The next morning, Annie awoke with a sense of excitement. Today, she would be returning home to visit her pa for the day—the first time she'd been away from Jed's ranch since arriving.

"It'll be odd having you away from the ranch for a day," Marvin said as he hitched the horses to the wagon. "I've kinda got used to having you around."

"Oh, that's a nice thing to say, Marvin," Annie responded, smiling broadly. "I kinda like being here n'all, but I'm looking forward to seeing my pa. It'll be good to have a day at home."

Marvin tipped his hat. "Well, just as long as you come back."

Billy appeared by their side. "I agree, Miss Annie. I ain't ever eaten so good since you came."

Annie laughed and looked at the pair of them. "I'll be back tonight. On my pa's life, I promise!"

“Alright then.” Marvin grinned, “Jed said I'm to bring you back afore sundown, so we’d better be on our way, so you get enough time with your pa."

Annie nodded, climbing up onto the wagon seat. As they set off, they passed Jed. He was standing by the front gate, fixing one of the posts. He stopped when he heard the wagon and turned to look at them.

“Have a good day, Annie.” He drawled.

“I will, Jed.” She smiled at him. “And thank you for the tobacco for Pa.”

He nodded his head and then said to Marvin, “No dillydallying at Annie’s. Do you hear?”

“No, sir.”

He turned back to his task, his big arms rippling with the weight of the hammer he held as he knocked the post into the hard ground. Even through his winter jacket, she could see the sheer strength of the man. Annie found she could hardly draw her eyes away. He was so strong.

She watched until the wagon took her out of his sight and then turned back to the pretty scenery unfolding before her. The snow wasn’t too thick, which was lucky; otherwise, she doubted she would have been going anywhere.

It was still cold though, and she hugged the blanket around her legs and waist. The air was fresh on her cheeks, but it didn’t matter. She was too excited about seeing her pa to even notice.

Marvin pulled the wagon to a halt outside the front of her house and a few minutes later,

her pa appeared, greeting her with a warm embrace.

"There's my girl!" he exclaimed. "I've missed yuh, Annie."

"I've missed you too, Pa," she replied, blinking back joyful tears.

She introduced Marvin to him, and he offered him a drink before he returned to the ranch, but Marvin declined.

"That's mighty kind of you, sir, but Jed instructed me to come straight back, and he's not a man to disobey!"

Annie shifted uncomfortably, remembering her spanking. Marvin was totally correct on that count!

"Oh, well. Next time then. Have a safe journey back." Her pa said.

As Marvin turned the wagon about and left for Jed's, Annie linked her arm through her pa's, and they walked inside the house.

She was pleased to see everything looked quite tidy. "You've kept everything nice, Pa, or was that down to Emmy?"

"Well, I didn't want yuh returnin' to a pigsty, Annie, and yes, Emmy gave me a bit of help." He smiled at her. "But I could do with some help in the barns."

"Of course. I'll go upstairs and get changed into some old clothes. I won't be a minute."

They spent the day working side-by-side—Annie helping with the milking, preparing a few hearty meals for her father, and tidying the small house. Throughout it all, her father asked about her new life on the ranch.

"So Jed's been treatin' yuh alright, then?" He inquired, his brow creased with concern.

"Yes, Pa, everything's just fine," Annie assured him. She saw no need to mention the curtain incident; she didn't want to worry him unnecessarily. Besides, she didn't want anyone to know that Jed had spanked her with his big old mean hands. Thinking of him made her say, "Which reminds me, he gave me some tobacco to give you."

She walked over to her bag and pulled out the pouch, handing it to him. His face lit up. "That's a grand gesture."

"I thought you'd appreciate it. Jed's not so bad when you get to know him. I know it's only been a week, but he doesn't seem so fearsome to me now." *Not unless I'm over his knee!* She thought to herself.

"No, he's a good man. I don't blame him for acting the way he has. He could've got the Marshal involved, and he didn't."

Annie pulled a face. "That's true." That would have been so embarrassing, having the town folk know about their money problems.

She looked out of the kitchen window as the sun began to sink low in the sky. It would soon be time to head back. "I'll make a coffee before I leave. Do you want a cup?"

Her pa nodded and seated himself at the kitchen table. "And one of those cookies you made. Danged if I can't wait to taste one," he laughed.

Whilst the coffee was brewing, Annie rushed upstairs to get changed back into her nice clothes, putting her others in the wash bag along with her pa's old clothes. She'd do them at Jed's and bring them back on her next visit.

A little while later, a knock came on the door, and Annie got up to open it, expecting Marvin, but instead Jed stood there, his big figure almost filling the doorframe.

"Oh!" Annie exclaimed.

"Evening, Annie," he greeted her, his deep voice rumbling. "I figured I'd come collect you myself, seeing as how this was your first trip home."

Annie blinked, momentarily caught off guard. "Did you think I wasn't going to come back? Didn't you trust me?" Her eyes sparkled with affrontery, thinking that he didn't know she was a woman of her word.

"No need to bristle, little girl." He drawled. "And no, I didn't think that at all."

She relaxed a little, realizing she may have been a bit hasty. "Oh, well... thank you, Jed. I appreciate that."

Jed merely nodded, his eyes looking past her to her father. "Evening, Abel."

"Jed."

"Would you like a coffee now you're here?" Annie asked him.

He declined, saying, “We should head back before it gets dark. Those clouds in the distance tell me more snow’s coming.”

“Oh, then I guess we’d better hurry!” She grabbed her bag and hugged her father tightly, promising to visit again soon.

"Take care of yourself, Annie," he said, pressing a gentle kiss to her forehead. "And I’ll see yuh next week."

"If you need me for anything, just get Emmy to send a message. Promise me, Pa," Annie said.

He nodded, and she added, "I love you, Pa."

Jed followed her outside and offered her a hand up into the wagon. As they set off back to the ranch, Annie couldn't help but wonder at Jed giving up his time to come and collect her.

The ride was quiet, save for the rhythmic clop of the horse's hooves. Annie stole occasional glances at him, but he kept his gaze fixed firmly on the road ahead. Just as the ranch came into view, he finally spoke.

"How was your day, little girl?" he asked gruffly.

"It was lovely; thank you," Annie replied. "It was so good to see my pa. But I'm glad to be back as well. I’m quite enjoying the challenge."

Jed's lips quirked in a faint smile. "Good to hear it. The hands have been lost without you, I reckon."

Annie felt a warm flutter in her chest at his words, and she laughed, “But I’ve only been gone a day!”

“You didn’t see what we had for lunch.”

Annie placed a hand over her mouth and giggled, “Was it that bad?”

“Uh-uh and then some.”

"Well, I'm happy to be of service, Jed. And thank you for coming to get me yourself. You didn't have to do that."

Jed simply grunted in response, but Annie thought she saw a glimmer of something akin to fondness in his handsome face. As they pulled up to the ranch house, she realised that she felt quite happy to be there.

Jed helped her down off the bench seat and placed her lightly on the ground, his eyes looking intently into hers.

"I know you must be a little tired after today," he said in a low tone, "but you couldn't rustle us all up a bit of supper, could you?"

"Of course." She smiled. In all truth she was tired, but it didn't take much effort to make a quick supper for them all. Also, even though he had every right to order her to make the meal—he hadn't, he'd asked.

So, quickly bustling inside, she set about preparing a meal, and half an hour later, the ranch hands and Jed were tucking into her food, their appreciative voices filling the kitchen amidst lip-smacking sounds.

She glanced at Jed, and he smiled back, raising his glass to her. "To Annie and her fine food."

"Amen to that!" the others said.

Annie went to bed that night with a smile on her face, and as soon as her head touched the pillow, she was fast asleep.

Chapter Five

During the next couple of weeks, Annie did her usual routine and visited her pa once a week. He seemed to be getting along just fine, and the widow, Emmy, who came to look in on him seemed to be making him happy. She was glad. It made her feel less worried than if he'd been entirely alone.

Life at Jed's ranch was going well. All the ranch hands loved her cooking and appreciated that she kept on top of the washing, giving them clean clothes and changing the bed sheets. It took up most of her time, but that was why she was there.

It was only a few days before Christmas, and Annie asked Jed if she could go home on Christmas day to spend time with her pa.

To her surprise, Jed refused. They were sitting alone at the breakfast table.

"What?" She said, looking at him in disbelief and wondering if she'd heard incorrectly.

"You heard me, Annie."

"Why are you being so unreasonable? I know it's a couple of days earlier than I'd usually go, but what does it matter?"

Jed tapped his fingers on the table, and then, with a heavy sigh, he eased himself up out of the chair and, grabbing her arm at the same time, lifted her up from her seat. He then gently propelled her towards the window and pointed outside.

"What do you see outside, Annie?"

"Snow."

"Yep, snow. Lots of snow. There ain't no way we're gonna be able to get the wagon out in that."

"I bet I could."

Jed chuckled. "Now who's being unreasonable?"

"I ain't! I've been through worse snow than that."

He raised a hand, stalling her. "You're not going, and that's that. Moan and whine all you like, but you ain't going!"

"But...!"

He shook his head. "Don't even think about it."

He gave her one last warning look, and then shrugging on his thick jacket and boots, he was gone.

Annie slapped her hand down on the table. "We'll see about that!" She hissed to herself. "Snow ain't gonna stop me from seeing my pa!"

At lunchtime, Jed entered the kitchen a little later than the others and noticed there was a decidedly frosty atmosphere in the room. Billy glanced at him, his eyes wide, and then darted a glance at Annie.

She was bustling about like she had a flea in her ear. It could only be for one reason. The fact that he'd denied her taking the wagon out.

The kitchen was thick with tension. Even Marvin was keeping quiet, and he was the most jovial. Annie walked over carrying a tray laden with plates and cups. Her features were set in a determined, almost defiant expression as she began serving the men their dinner.

Jed watched her with a raised brow, and when she'd finished, he couldn't help but notice that his portion seemed a bit smaller than the others, and when Annie poured his coffee, it was decidedly lukewarm.

"Thank you, Annie," Jed said gruffly, eyeing her thoughtfully.

"You're welcome," Annie replied, keeping her tone clipped and formal.

Jed glanced down at his plate. "Something wrong with my supper tonight?"

"Not at all. There's plenty to go around," Annie responded, her gaze meeting his defiantly. "What's wrong with it?"

"It just seems I have less than everyone else, and my coffee seems a bit on the cool side. You feeling alright? Something bothering you?" Jed pressed, knowing full well what it was.

"I'm just fine, Jed. Perfectly fine," Annie said stubbornly.

Marvin, ever the peacekeeper, quickly interjected. "Uh, this sure is a fine meal, Annie. Best cookin' you've done so far, I'd say."

Annie's expression softened slightly as she acknowledged Marvin's compliment. "Thank you, Marvin. I'm glad *you're* enjoying it." And then her eyes flashed back to Jed's, her lips tight.

Jed let out a long drawn sigh, set down his cup, and leaned back in his chair. "Now, Annie, I know you're still sore about me saying you can't go home for Christmas. But you have to understand, you simply can't take the wagon out in that amount of snow."

Annie dug her heels in. "I could!" She looked at Billy, trying to get support. "Ain't that right, Billy?"

Billy looked from one to the other and wisely decided to keep out of the argument. "Well, I, errr..." He scratched his head. "I gotta get back to work!"

He quickly left the room, and the others swiftly followed. Annie watched the door slam shut and huffed loudly.

Lifting a placating hand, Jed replied, "I know it ain't easy, Annie. Your pa will understand."

"I should be able to visit him, just for the one day," Annie insisted stubbornly.

Jed's tone left no room for argument. "My decision stands, Annie. You're staying put. Now sit and eat your dinner before it gets any colder."

Annie shot Jed a resentful look but reluctantly took her seat, picking at her food with a sullen expression.

Annie did the washing up with gusto. Trying to get rid of her temper, but it didn't work. She hated being denied anything, especially when she was damn sure she could take that wagon out. Yes, the snow was thick, but nothing her horses weren't used to.

Maybe Jed's weren't used to being out in that much snow? But if hers could do it, so could his.

Stalking up to her bedroom, she threw herself on the bed and thumped the pillow. God, he was so overbearing. What gave him leave to think he could tell her what to do?

Standing up from the bed, she walked over to the window to look out at the view. The snow looked so pretty, sparkling against the sun. Sure, it was thick, but in her eyes, that wasn't a problem. She suddenly spied Jed walking just below her window.

Narrowing her eyes, an idea came to mind, and before she knew what she was doing, she opened the window and called down to him.

"Jed? Oh, Jed?"

He stopped walking and looked up. "What is it Annie?"

"I have something for you." Her temper high, she picked up her pitcher of water and, leaning out of the window, emptied the whole lot over his head.

It drenched him, and she laughed loudly before slamming the window back shut. Clapping a hand over her mouth, she quickly rushed over to her door to lock it, but then, in horror, she remembered there was no lock! *Damnation!*

She looked around the room frantically and ran over to the only chair, dragging it across the room—her thought process to try and block out Jed if he decided to exact revenge. She wasn't even half way over before the door burst open, and he stood there, his hair plastered to his head and a look of thunder on his face.

Annie screamed and tried to dive under the bed, but his hand was around her ankle in an instant.

"Oh, no, you don't! You conniving little madam."

She tried kicking her legs and pushing herself forward, but Jed's strength meant she had no chance. No chance at all. He pulled her out in front of him, rolled her over, and hunkered down next to her.

"You're a spoiled little madam, do you know that?"

"Jed! I can explain! I was just a little angry and didn't realise what I was doing." She couldn't help the bubble of laughter that burst forth as she looked at the drips of water running down his face. Her eyes sparkled with delicious revenge. That would teach him for trying to control her.

"You knew exactly what you were doing." He replied, his eyes darkening. "Well, guess what, Annie. So do I!" He grabbed her wrist and pulled her upright. She had a feeling she knew what was coming and struggled like fury to break free. But of course, it didn't work.

He settled himself on her bed, and the next instant she was over his lap, her bottom high and her hands scraping the floor.

"Please, Jed, I didn't mean it."

"Oh, yes, you did. By God, you've got a temper on you." He threw her skirts over her back. "But I have a great way of deterring that sort of behaviour."

She felt him part her bloomers, and then his massive palm impacted on her little bottom.

"*Ow!*" She yelped. "This ain't fair!"

"Oh, yes, it is. I'm freezin' to the bone 'cause of you. When I've finished spanking your butt, you're gonna go and fetch me some new clothes, do you hear?"

He brought his hand crashing down on her buttocks again, the impact moving her forward and illicting a high-pitched wail. "*Oooooh!*"

His hand came down again and again with no let-up. He sure was angry. She felt the familiar burn as he heated up her tender buttocks to sizzling point. Hot damn. She wasn't going to be sitting comfortably again. When would she ever learn?

"*Ouch! Oh!*" She cried, screwing up her face in pain. "Please stop! I won't ever do it again!"

"No, you won't. I'm going to make sure of it." He growled, smacking both buttocks at the same time.

"*Ooooh!*"

Finally, when she thought she couldn't take anymore, he stopped, leaving his palm covering one whole cheek. Even though her backside was like a furnace, she couldn't help feeling a stirring of desire at his touch. The feeling of laying over his firm thighs and his big arm holding her tight against his muscular body was doing peculiar things to her nether regions and her tummy.

She chewed her bottom lip, wondering what in the hell she was thinking!

Jed's jaw clenched as he looked down at his handiwork on Annie's naughty bottom. It was the least she deserved. With a temper like that, she was destined to be put over his lap more often than not, but he had to admit, he enjoyed it. The feel of her soft little butt beneath his fingertips was warming to say the least, and watching the soft flesh jiggle on impact was a sight for sore eyes.

So, in all truth, he didn't mind at all. The naughtier she was, the more he'd have to chastise her.

But he wasn't finished with her yet. She needed to apologise.

"I think you owe me an apology." He said, his tone low.

"You've just spanked me, ain't that enough?" She spat, trying to rise up.

He kept his hand firmly on her back. "Uh-uh, little girl. You dang well know it ain't. And just to let you know, if you don't apologise, I'm gonna take you right out front and put your bare butt in the snow. I don't care who's around or who sees. Understand?"

He heard her gasp and closed his eyes to quell the laughter that threatened to burst forth. Two could play at her game.

"Well, I...!"

"What was that, Annie?"

"I'm sorry, alright," she bit out. "I shouldn't have thrown the water like that."

He nodded to himself and reluctantly drew her bloomers together, hiding her pretty little tush from his gaze. He pulled her skirts down and finally let her up. She rose up quickly, clasping her hands on her bottom and shooting him a sullen look, but he noted she didn't look quite as defiant as earlier.

He pointed at the door. "Go get me some clean clothes, Annie. I'll be in my bedroom."

He gave her a stern look and then, striding to the door, left her room.

Annie stared after him, softly rubbing her hot derriere. Damned cowboy! Now she couldn't concentrate properly. Not only was her backside on fire, her emotions were all askew. That was twice now he'd spanked her. What sort of man was he?

Tall. Handsome. Swoonworthy.

She pursed her lips, instantly reprimanding herself out loud. "Don't start getting all doe-eyed over him, Annie! He ain't worth it!"

She stomped out of the room and down the stairs to the laundry area. Some of his clothes were hanging up drying. Grabbing a pair of trousers and a clean shirt, she stomped back up the stairs and headed for his bedroom.

Without thinking, she threw the door open and then stopped dead in her tracks. He was butt naked with his back to her.

"Oh!" She gasped, quickly turning around. "Pardon me!"

She heard him laugh, a deep rumble in his chest. “Don’t mind me, Annie. Come on in.”

“I won’t thank you! Not until you’re decent!”

She suddenly froze when she heard him right behind her. He snaked a hand around her front and reached for the clothes she was holding. “I’ll take those.” She looked down at his large hand and shivered slightly. He was so big and masculine, she could see his forearms rippling with his toned muscles. She couldn't help but feast her eyes on them, and then annoyed with herself, she almost ran from the room.

She heard his deep laughter behind her and narrowed her eyes as she high-tailed it down the stairs. Lord, that man was getting under her skin!

Chapter Six

By Christmas Eve, Annie was surprised to find herself looking forward to the holiday, even so far from home. But she was still sad she couldn't see her pa.

The morning had brought a fresh blanket of snow on the ground, putting paid to any thoughts she might have had that would change Jed's mind. There wasn't a hope in hell now.

She finished her chores after breakfast and was resting by the fire, sewing one of Billy's shirts, when Jed came in from the barn.

"I made some coffee, if you want one." Annie told him. He gave a curt nod and sat down at the kitchen table. As she prepared his drink, she couldn't help but notice that he seemed distracted, his thoughts elsewhere. He wasn't talking, but then he was a man of few words at the best of times.

She placed the mug in front of him and sat down opposite. "Is something troubling you, Jed?"

She watched his hand curl into a fist on the table. "Bill Hannon, my neighbour, visited me this morning and told me he spoke to the Marshal a couple of days ago. He told him that Mary was in town."

"Your sister?"

He nodded, his face grave. "More to the point, she was on her own."

"Oh!" Annie said, "Do you think she's run away from her husband?"

Jed raised his eyes to hers, "If she even married him."

Annie gasped. "What're you going to do—bring her back here?" She stood up and walked over to the window, looking outside. "But then you can't, can you... because of the snow. I can't even get to visit my pa."

"That's what's so damn frustrating, Annie."

She turned from the window and laid a hand on his shoulder. He naturally reached a hand up to cover hers. It was a moment of shared intimacy that neither of them had anticipated and seemed to startle them.

Jed removed his hand and clearing his throat, said, "All I can do is wait for the dang snow to clear, but who knows when that'll be? I just hope she hasn't done anything stupid. If they ain't married and she's with child, god help me. I'll kill him with my bare hands."

Annie's eyes widened seeing the sincerity in his face. Lord. She almost pitied the salesman, but then if he had done that, then he deserved to be punished. Maybe not death, but definitely something. Although, judging by Jed's fierce expression, maybe he wouldn't get a choice!

"Do you know where she's staying?" Annie asked him.

"Marshal said he saw her with Milly Adams. She runs a guesthouse, so I can only assume she's staying there." He gave a heavy sigh. "At least she's got a roof over her head until this snow clears."

He finished his coffee and stood up. "I'll get back to work."

He shrugged on his coat and boots before turning to look at her. "I'm real sorry you ain't seeing your pa, Annie."

She smiled. "Thank you, Jed. That means a lot."

She watched him go back out into the snow, and when the door closed behind him, she sat down again at the table. Well, one thing was for sure. Just because she couldn't see her pa, she was still going to put on a lovely spread and enjoy this Christmas. Hopefully it would cheer Jed up as well.

Christmas Day

Annie awoke early, excited to spend the day with Jed and the ranch hands. She threw her bedroom curtains open and looked out across the crisp, snow-covered fields. It might be stopping her plans, but there was no denying how pretty it looked.

Dressing in her prettiest outfit, a pale blue cotton dress with a white lace collar and intricate embroidered flowers, she brushed her hair until it shone, pinning part of it up with matching blue hair clips. Pinching her cheeks to give them colour, she rushed downstairs to begin breakfast, throwing on her apron to keep herself as clean as she could.

As she bustled about the kitchen, with the aroma of freshly brewed coffee filling the air, the ranch hands began stirring. Luke was the first one to appear, scratching his head and yawning.

"Morning, Luke. Merry Christmas." Annie grinned at him.

"And to you, Annie."

He took a seat at the table, and she poured him a coffee. "Breakfast won't be long."

The rest of the ranch hands appeared, one by one, and all took a seat. Billy still looked half asleep. "Didn't you sleep well, Billy?" She asked him.

"Not really, Miss Annie. My head was hurting."

Marvin nudged him with his elbow, laughing. "That's because you drank too much of that whisky last night. I told you to slow down a bit!"

"Oh-ho!" said Jed walking into the room and overhearing their conversation. "Drinking on the job, eh, Billy?" He shook his head, smiling. "Lucky for you, I'm feeling lenient as it's Christmas."

"I didn't have much, honest, Jed."

"I believe you." He laughed, taking a seat. "Morning, Annie," He said, a smile spreading across his face as his eyes met hers. "Merry Christmas."

"Morning, Jed," Annie replied, returning his smile. "Since we can't make it to church with all this snow, I thought I'd read a passage from the Bible to us all after dinner. And I've got a special meal planned, with some mulled wine afterwards to warm us up."

Jed's eyes lit up. "Mulled wine! Well, ain't that just the perfect way to spend Christmas on the ranch?" He chuckled, slapping Luke on the back. "I can already taste the rich, spiced aroma."

The other ranch hands nodded in agreement, their faces brightening at the prospect of Annie's festive feast. "That sounds wonderful, Annie," Danny said. "I'm mighty grateful to have you here with us; no one cooks as good as you."

Annie beamed at the compliment. It was nice to be appreciated. She placed a big pot of scrambled eggs on the table, a big plate of bacon, and another of bread. "Well, then, you'd better get stuck in! I've got a lot of cooking to do, and I want to make sure we all have a Christmas to remember."

After the meal, when they'd all left to do their chores, she started clearing the dishes, humming to herself. She stopped for a moment, realising how normal all this seemed to her now. Smiling, she piled the dishes in the sink and waited for the water to boil so she could clean them.

She heard Jed clearing his throat behind her; she wouldn't mistake that low rumble, so she turned around to look at him.

"I, uh, got something for you," he said. He was holding a parcel in his hands. He walked over and handed it to her.

"Oh, you got me a present!" Annie exclaimed. She quickly unwrapped it to find a knitted shawl, the richest blue wool she'd ever seen. "Oh, Jed, it's beautiful! But I have nothing to give you," she said shyly.

He waved off her concern. "Your hard work these past weeks is a gift enough. Ranch ain't been so clean and cheery in awhile." His eyes met hers, and in that moment Annie realized how much she liked him.

Her heart fluttered, and on impulse, she placed her hands on his shoulders and, standing on tiptoe, kissed his cheek. "Thank you, Jed. I love it," she beamed. To her surprise, Jed smiled back, his eyes crinkling with genuine pleasure. "I'll wear it after dinner."

He looked down at her, and it seemed like he was going to say something else, but then he simply said, "I'm glad you like it, Annie."

Jed left Annie to begin the preparations for dinner and made his way outside into the snow. When she'd kissed his cheek just now, the compunction to throw his arms around her and kiss her thoroughly was an urge he'd had to fight. She looked so beautiful and innocent, standing there, her face all lit up with excitement.

He cursed under his breath. What was he thinking? What would she want with an old cowboy like him? He was thirty-six, much older than her twenty-three.

And one thing he kept forgetting: she was only here to pay her father's debt. It wasn't out of the goodness of her heart. Who in their right mind would choose to live on a ranch and cook for a load of men every day?

He sighed and rubbed his forehead as he strode towards the barns. He'd known for a while now that he had feelings for her. Who wouldn't? She might be a sassy little baggage, but that's exactly what he was looking for. He admired that in a woman. A bit of spunk.

No weak-willed, dainty woman would suit him. She wouldn't stand a chance on this ranch. Why, she wouldn't even last one damn day!

He laughed to himself, feeling the cheer of Christmas ripple through him at the thought of the meal Annie was preparing. Well, even if she didn't feel the same way, at least he still had her for another couple of months, and he was going to damn well make sure he enjoyed every minute.

Annie rang the bell, just outside the kitchen door, to inform everyone dinner was ready. The ranch hands and Jed filed into the kitchen, their faces flushed from the crisp winter air and the morning's chores. Annie stood at the head of the table, her new blue shawl draped elegantly over her shoulders and her eyes sparkling as she watched their expressions as they all surveyed the spread before them.

The table was laden, and even though it had taken her ages, she was very proud of it all. A golden-brown roasted turkey took center stage, its savory aroma mingling with the scent of fresh-baked bread and the earthy fragrance of roasted root vegetables. She'd also made a hearty beef stew and creamy mashed potatoes. Something for everyone.

Jed's eyes lit up as he looked at it all. "Well, Annie, you've done yourself proud, I must say, and the shawl looks lovely on you." He said, his voice warm with appreciation.

Annie beamed, liking the fact that he'd noticed. "Thank you, Jed. Now everyone sit down; we'll say grace, and then you can tuck in as you like."

After the last morsel had been eaten, they all retired to the living room, settling into the cosy armchairs and sofas. It had started to snow again, and Billy added an extra log to the fire to keep everyone warm.

Annie poured out steaming mugs of mulled wine, the rich, spiced aroma filling the room. As the fire crackled and the ranch hands sipped their drinks, Annie opened the well-worn Bible and began to read as promised, her voice soft and soothing.

Just as she finished the passage, a loud knock came on the door, echoing through the room. Annie frowned and looked at Jed. "Are you expecting someone?"

Jed shook his head and rose from his seat, his brow furrowed with concern. "Who's come knocking in this weather?"

He opened the door, and Annie heard him gasp with surprise. "Mary?"

There, on the threshold stood his sister, Mary, her face pale and her lips tinged with blue. "Jed..." she gasped, collapsing into his arms, frozen to the core.

"What the heck!" He exclaimed, quickly bringing her inside.

Annie was right behind him. "What in tarnation is she doing out in this weather? She can't have walked from town. Can she?"

"Get a blanket, would you, Annie?" Jed said quickly. "She's freezing."

Annie sped to the laundry room and quickly found the thickest blanket she could. Rushing back, she gave it to Jed. He had already laid his sister on the couch, the boys quickly standing aside to make room for her.

Jed wrapped the blanket around her and stroked her face. "Mary? Mary?"

She moaned a little, but her eyes remained closed.

"She looks awful white, Jed." Marvin said. "I'll stoke the fire a bit, get some more heat goin'."

Annie handed Jed a fresh glass of mulled wine. "Get that down her, Jed."

He raised her head a little and put the glass to her lips, pouring a little into her mouth. She swallowed it and began to cough. "Oh!" she breathed and finally opened her eyes. She focussed on Jed and quickly put her arms around him. "Oh, Jed. It's so good to be home!"

"What in tarnation were you thinking, running off like that?" Jed said, his voice gruff.

He was thrilled to have her back home again, but at the same time he was angry at the way she'd behaved. He realised though, that for now he would have to hold his tongue. Not only didn't he want to ruin the lovely atmosphere, but he didn't want to scold his sister in front of the ranch hands.

Mary's eyes met his, a silent plea for understanding. "I'm sorry, Jed. I just couldn't stay there any longer. That man, he..." She shuddered, the memory clearly still fresh in her mind.

Jed let out a heavy sigh and placed a large hand on her shoulder. "We'll talk about it later. Right now, you need to rest." He turned to Annie, his gaze softening. "Annie, would you mind showing Mary to her old room? I think she could use some quiet and warmth."

Annie nodded, her expression kind. "Of course, Jed." They helped Mary to her feet, and Annie put her arm around her, gently guiding her up the stairs.

In the cozy bedroom, Annie pulled back the freshly laundered sheets and, after helping Mary out of her wet clothes, assisted her into a fresh nightgown from one of the drawers. Mary climbed onto the bed, and Annie quickly drew the covers over her to keep her warm.

Mary snuggled down, a grateful smile tugging at the corners of her lips. "Thank you, Annie, isn't it? I'm sorry, but I don't even know who you are."

Annie smiled. "It's a long story, but I'm here to help your brother out for a few months. My name's Annie Johnson."

Mary returned the smile, and Annie could see in her eyes that she was sincere. Eyes that looked just like her brothers.

"Do you want to rest or would you prefer some company?" Annie asked.

"I think I'd like to sleep for a while if you don't mind. It's been a long day."

With a reassuring squeeze to her hand, Annie left the room, closing the door softly behind her.

Walking back down the stairs, she wondered what on earth had happened to make her walk all the way from town back to the ranch. Had she married the salesman, and more to the point, was she still innocent, or had the cad had his wicked way with her?

One thing was certain: Jed wasn't a man to sit idly by and let someone take advantage of his sister. She knew that as sure as apples were apples! Tomorrow was going to be interesting!

She made her way into the living area to find that the ranch hands were no longer there. "Where's everyone gone?" She asked Jed, sitting back down.

Jed was standing by the fireplace, staring down into the flames, and he turned to look at her. "They thought it better to celebrate in their quarters. Give Mary a little peace." He gave her a wry smile. "How is she?"

"She wants to sleep. Perhaps in the morning, we'll know more." She shrugged her slender shoulders. "She doesn't seem so cold now. I think a good night's rest will do her the world of good."

Jed crossed his arms over his broad chest. "I had a gut feeling something like this would happen. Men like Evan don't hang around for long." His jaw tightened. "If he's taken advantage of her, I'm gonna make him regret the day he was born."

"We don't know that yet, Jed." Annie said quietly. "Maybe they never got to that point."

"Maybe. Maybe not. But either way, he's still gonna have me to answer to, one way or another."

Annie nodded. She wouldn't like to be Evan Wallis when Jed got hold of him. No siree!

Chapter Seven

The next morning

Annie knocked gently on Mary's bedroom door, a tray laden with a hearty breakfast balanced in her hands. "Mary? It's Annie. I've brought you some food, if you're feeling up to it."

She had already served the others breakfast and thought that Mary might appreciate the privacy of having hers in her own room, away from questioning eyes.

She was surprised when the door creaked open, and Mary appeared, her expression a little weary but definitely looking perkier than yesterday. She had the quilt wrapped around her shoulders.

"Oh, Annie, you're too kind."

"I thought you'd still be in bed." Annie said, bustling past her. "Are you sure you feel well enough to get up?"

She placed the tray down on the small table and noticed Mary's eyes light up at the sight of the steaming coffee and freshly cooked bread and eggs.

"I feel so much better." Mary said, "I've never been so cold as last night, Annie. It went right through to my bones."

She sat down at the table, moving one arm from beneath the quilt to reach for a fork, and began tucking into the eggs. "These are delicious."

Annie smiled happily. Mary's desire to eat was a clear sign that she had significantly recovered from the previous night. Things could have been so much worse.

Annie moved to the bed and began to neaten the covers and plump the pillows. She was dying to ask Mary what had happened but wasn't sure if it was her place. Her curiosity was driving her mad, though.

Biting her lip, she decided to just come out with it. She walked back over to the table and said, "Jed mentioned that you, err, eloped with a salesman. You don't have to tell me, but what happened to make you come back?"

Mary hesitated for a moment, then let out a heavy sigh. "Well, the truth is, Annie... Evan and I, well, we did get married." She averted her gaze, her cheeks flushing with embarrassment.

Annie's eyes widened in surprise, but she quickly composed herself. "So where is he now?"

Mary's eyes darkened. "In hell for all I care!"

Annie nibbled on a fingernail. "Don't you love him anymore?"

"No! And I ain't ever going back to him either."

"Good lord, what did he do?"

"He treated me awfully, Annie. I never expected a husband to act like that." She thrust out her bottom lip. "Marrying him was a mistake, a terrible one. Evan, he—he wasn't the man I thought he was. He acted so badly, and I just couldn't bear it anymore. That's why I ran away."

Annie had heard about men beating on their women and just didn't understand it. But hearing the distress in Mary's voice saddened her. She reached out and squeezed Mary's hand, her expression filled with compassion. "I'm so sorry you had to go through that. You must've been so frightened."

Mary nodded, her eyes glistening with unshed tears. "I was, Annie. But I'm grateful to be back home. I don't know what I would've done if I hadn't found my way back here."

Annie patted her shoulder. "To be honest, in that snow, I don't know how you even did! But you're safe now. We're here for you, no matter what." She moved the coffee cup towards her. "Have some coffee; it'll warm you up.

She watched as Mary sipped on the hot brew, her expression full of self-pity. What on earth had Evan done to her?

"You'll have to get a divorce." Annie reasoned, "You can't stay married to such a brute. The Marshal should be able to help you with that. Either way, your brother will help you, I'm certain." She looked at her reassuringly. "You can start over then."

A tear slipped down Mary's face, and Annie frowned. "What is it?"

Mary swallowed hard and said quietly, "It ain't gonna be that simple. You see... I'm gonna have a baby."

"Oh!"

Jed sipped on his coffee whilst thinking about his sister. She'd always been troublesome, always wanting her own way and, more often than not, getting it. Their father had always been too soft on her. Even though she'd received his belt a couple of times, it should've been more, in his humble opinion. She might not have turned out so flighty then.

Running away with Evan had been a really dumb move to take. But now she was back, and although he was pleased to have her home, he also knew something wasn't right. What on earth had happened for her to traipse all that way in the thick snow? She could have died out there in the cold.

He sipped his coffee, thinking hard. He'd only met Evan a few times, and he'd seemed a pretty decent fellow. Annoying he had to say, but most salesmen annoyed him, and he was a bit full of himself, but that happened sometimes with the young'uns. They fancied themselves a bit more than the next man. It only needed someone to take them down a peg or two and usually they fit right in.

Only Mary had eloped with him before he'd had the chance, and then, of course, he'd just wanted to kill him.

He looked up as Annie entered the kitchen. Her brow was furrowed, and he knew instantly something wasn't right. "What is it? Is Mary alright? Do I need to send for the doctor?"

"No, no. She's fine." Annie took a seat opposite him, looking troubled.

"What is it then? You can tell me." Jed said.

"Oh, I don't know if it's my place to say something, Jed. I think you'd best hear it from your sister directly."

"Is she up for receiving visitors?"

"Yes, but go easy on her, Jed."

Jed mounted the stairs and knocked gently on the bedroom door. "Mary? You up for talking?"

He heard her answer, "Jed, of course. Come in."

Jed stepped into the room, his brow furrowed with concern. He noticed she had colour in her cheeks and looked a whole lot better than yesterday. She was still sipping on the coffee Annie had given her, and he was pleased to see the empty plates on the tray.

"Annie told me you two had a talk this morning. Now, I gotta ask—what in the blazes were you thinking running here like that in the middle of a blizzard? You could've frozen to death out there!"

Mary averted her gaze, her fingers fidgeting with the quilt. "I know, Jed, I know. But I... I couldn't stay with Evan any longer. He-" She paused, swallowing hard. "He hit me, Jed. I wasn't going to stay married to a man like that, no matter what."

"He hit you?" A surge of anger ripped through him so hard that his hands curled into fists. "I'm going to kill him!"

"Don't do anything like that, Jed! I don't want you getting into trouble over him. He ain't worth it."

Jed closed his eyes for a moment, trying to curb his anger, but it was hard. So Evan had actually made an honest woman out of her but then thought that gave him leave to treat her any way he liked. If he walked in the room now, Jed wouldn't be responsible for his actions.

He walked over to Mary and placed his calloused hand on her arm. "I can't promise I won't hit him, but one thing's for sure: you did the right thing in getting yourself out of that situation. I'll have a talk with the Marshal; see what can be done about getting you a divorce."

Mary nodded, a glimmer of relief in her eyes. "Thank you, Jed. I just want to put this whole mess behind me."

Jed gave her arm a gentle squeeze. "You know I'll do anything to help you." He paused, his brow furrowing once more. "But I still don't understand why you eloped in the first place."

"Well, I knew you didn't like Evan all that much."

"I never said I didn't like him," Jed defended himself.

"Well, you often said he was full of himself."

"Well, sure he was. I was just saying the plain truth, Mary. I know you were sweet on him, but I did try and tell you not to go off with him."

She shrugged her shoulders. "I dunno, Jed. I guess I should've listened to you.

"Damn right, you should have!" Jed admonished her. He tapped his fingers on the table with frustration and then added, "But what's done is done, I guess. At least now, you can move on. And this time find a man that's decent, would you?"

He stood up and went to leave, but Mary caught his arm. "There's something else, Jed. I don't quite know how to say it, but... I'm going to have a baby."

Jed's eyes widened in surprise, and he whirled around to stare at her, running a hand through his thick hair. "A baby, huh? Well, I'll be..." He let out a heavy sigh. "I reckon that changes things a bit, doesn't it?"

Mary nodded, her eyes downcast. "I'm sorry, Jed. I know this must be a lot to take in."

Jed reached out and took her hand. "Well, it's happened now. We just have to deal with it. Same as we deal with anything that comes our way. Now, take it easy today; stay in bed and keep warm. Annie'll bring you up some dinner later."

Mary's eyes filled with tears, and she squeezed Jed's hand in return. "Thank you, Jed. I don't know what I'd do without you."

Jed gave her a reassuring smile. "That's what family's for, Mary. We'll get through this, one step at a time."

He left her alone, closing the bedroom door behind him. Well, a baby! Dang!

Over the next few days, Mary started helping Annie with the chores; but Annie wasn't comfortable with it and kept telling her to sit down because of her pregnancy.

"Oh, it's early days yet. "Mary said, looking down at her stomach. "The bump don't even show yet."

"Yes, but you still have to be careful, Mary." Annie admonished her.

"But I like helping you. It's not easy doing everything on your own. I should know."

Annie placed her hands on her hips. "Well, in all truth, it does make life a lot easier, but only if you're sure. Any pains, and you're to sit straight down!"

Mary laughed. "You're like the sister I never had."

The two of them got on like a house on fire, both finding they had a lot of things in common. In the evening, they took turns to read out loud, much to Jed's delight.

A week went by and the snow started to lessen, so Jed decided to take the wagon into town to see the Marshal about getting a divorce for Mary.

He got the boys to hitch the horses to the wagon and walked out the front, ready to leave. Annie ran up to him and handed him a note. "Can you get these, please, Jed? We're running low on a few things."

"Sure will."

He noticed his sister was standing by the door, her arms crossed over her chest, and looking a little nervous. He settled his eyes on her. "What's wrong, Mary?"

"Nothin'!"

"Don't tell me that. It's as plain as the nose on your face that you ain't happy about something, so spit it out."

She rolled her eyes. "I'm not sure I want to divorce him yet. I mean, I think I should talk to him first."

Jed raised an eyebrow and took a step back. "The man hit you, and you want to go back to him? Have you lost your senses, girl?"

Her lips thinned as her temper began to flare. Jed knew the signs. "I dunno what I want to do, Jed." Her bottom lip began to tremble, and she ran back inside the house and high-tailed it upstairs.

Annie stood by his side, her mouth a little O of surprise.

"What in tarnation has got into her?" Jed said out loud.

"Maybe it's her condition. I've heard that when a woman gets pregnant, they can act kinda funny."

Jed scratched his head. "Well, I'll leave you to sort her out, Annie. I'll speak with the Marshal anyhow." He placed his hand on her chin and raised her face to his. "You're a good girl, Annie."

He noticed a blush steal over her cheeks, and she gave him a cheeky smile. "Most of the time, Jed."

Laughing, he stepped up onto the bench seat, and with a flick of the reins, the wagon began to roll towards the gates. He turned around to find Annie staring after him, and it gladdened his heart.

Turning back around, he directed his thoughts towards the Marshal and what he was going to say to him.

When Jed arrived at the Marshal's office, he greeted him warmly, clapping him on the back. "Jed, I'm glad you're here. I was going to come out and see you this afternoon, so that saves me the trouble! I've got some news about your sister."

Jed nodded. "Before you say anything. She's back home."

"Already? I only heard this morning that she was back in town, but then she also went on the missing persons list." He sat down, scratching his head. "I can't keep up with all this!"

"Who reported her missing? Was it Evan?" Jed's look turned fierce.

The Marshal nodded solemnly. "He showed up in town just this morning, asking about her. He's staying at the local inn, and he's none too happy about her running off, I can tell you."

Jed clenched his jaw, his hands balling into fists. "Well, I know where I'm heading."

The Marshal raised a hand, trying to calm him down. "Now, Jed, I know you're upset, but you need to handle this carefully. He is her husband, after all, and he's already told me that he intends to go to your place to fetch Mary back."

Jed's eyes narrowed. "The hell he is! That man ain't laying a hand on my sister ever again, you hear me?"

The Marshal nodded, understanding the protective fury in Jed's voice. "I figured you'd feel that way, but remember to stay on the right side of the law. I don't fancy having to arrest you. Know what I mean?"

Jed let out a heavy sigh, running a hand through his hair. "Much obliged, Marshal. I'll handle this myself. That man ain't gonna get within a mile of my ranch, not if I have anything to say about it."

Without another word, Jed turned and strode out of the office, his mind determined. He just had to keep his temper under control, and that all depended on how Evan reacted to him.

Jed stormed into the inn, his eyes burning with fury as he glanced around the room looking for Evan.

Hank was behind the bar, cleaning a glass. He called over to him. "You looking for someone, Jed?"

Jed strode over to him. "Evan Wallis. You seen him?"

Hank nodded and eyed him warily. "You ain't gonna kill him, are you, Jed?"

Jed closed his eyes for a moment, calming his temper. "Nope. I just want to talk with him." He might beat him to a pulp, but he had no intention of actually killing him. Yet.

"Room eight-one-nine."

Taking the stairs two at a time, Jed soon found himself outside the room Evan was staying in. Raising his hand, he knocked loudly on the door. It didn't take long before the door opened.

Without a moment's hesitation, Jed grabbed Evan by the scruff of his neck and slammed him against the wall.

"You listen to me, you good for nothing bastard," Jed growled, his face mere inches from Evan's. "If you so much as lay a finger on my sister again, I'll make sure you never see the light of day, do you hear?"

Evan's eyes widened in fear, but then a look of defiance crossed his features. "Now, hold on just a minute, Jed. You've got it all wrong."

"Have I? I don't think so!"

"You've only heard her side of the story. All I did was give Mary a little... discipline, that's all."

Jed's grip tightened, his knuckles turning white. "Discipline? You call beating on a woman 'discipline'?"

Evan raised his hands in a placating gesture, and his voice a little raspy from lack of oxygen said, "Look, Jed, let's not get carried away here. Mary, she... she slapped me first, you see. I was simply putting her in her place, like any man has a right to do with his wife."

Jed's grip loosened ever so slightly, his expression shifting from rage to confusion. "What in the blazes are you talking about?"

Evan straightened his shirt nervously. "All I did was give her a good, old-fashioned spanking. Nothing more. She was being disrespectful, and I had to show her who's in charge."

Jed's grip slackened, and he took a step back, his mind reeling. "A spanking? That's it?"

Evan nodded. "That's it. I don't know what she told you, but that's all I did. I turned her over my knee and blistered her backside."

Jed stood there, stunned, as the reality of the situation sank in. He let out a heavy sigh and released his hold on Evan. "Goddamn. Let's take this downstairs and have a civilized talk, shall we?"

Evan nodded, looking very relieved. "Sure. It's something we've needed to do for a while."

Chapter Eight

As Annie bustled about the kitchen, making preparations for the evening meal, she couldn't help but notice how restless Mary was. She paced back and forth, her eyes constantly flickering towards the window. So much so that Annie had to ask her what was wrong.

"Mary, what's got you so worked up? You're wearing a hole in the floor." Annie said.

Mary paused midstep, wringing her hands nervously. "Oh, Annie, I'm just so worried about Jed talking to Evan. I... I haven't exactly been truthful about what happened between us."

Annie's brow furrowed, and she gestured for Mary to take a seat at the kitchen table. "What do you mean? What happened?"

Mary sank into the chair, her gaze downcast and looking almost guilty. "Well, the thing is... Evan didn't exactly hit me. He... he only spanked me for being disrespectful."

Annie's eyes widened. "Huh? But when you said he hit you, I thought you meant like a punch or something."

Mary nodded, her cheeks flushing with embarrassment. "I know. I was just so mad at him, so I sort of lied."

Annie sat back in her chair, feeling quite shocked. "Oh, Lord, Mary. You're going to be in so much trouble with Jed when he finds out."

Mary winced, "What am I gonna do?"

“I haven’t a clue. I’ve already managed to get into trouble twice with your brother. Both times he spanked me. He’s not a man who takes disobedience lightly, is he?”

Mary's head snapped up, her eyes wide with surprise. "You mean... you mean Jed has done that to you, too?"

Annie nodded, a wry smile tugging at the corners of her lips. "Oh, yes. I’m learning to behave, but it's hard."

Mary sat in stunned silence, her mind racing. "I... I had no idea. I always thought Jed was so understanding."

Annie chuckled softly. "Oh, he is. But that doesn't mean he won't put his foot down when he needs to. Perhaps that’s how Evan is. What happened for him to spank you, if you don’t mind me asking?”

Mary pulled a face. “I slapped him around the face.”

Annie gasped, “What did you do that for?”

“It weren’t nothin’ really. I suppose I shouldn’t have done it, but my temper got the better of me. He accused me of being flippant, Annie. Me, flippant!”

“In what context?” Anne had to ask.

"Well, I was tidying up the house and throwing things out, like you do. He found out that I’d thrown a big, ugly old vase out and that it had belonged to his gramma. How was I supposed to know that?”

Annie chewed her lip, trying to stifle a laugh. “Maybe by asking?”

Mary looked at her. “It is kinda funny, isn’t it? But his spanking certainly wasn’t. He went on about the damn vase so much that I just lost my temper and slapped him around the face, and that was when he grabbed me and threw me over his knee.” She paused, her face growing dark. “I ain’t ever had a spanking off him, Annie. It hurt like jeepers. So I packed a bag and high-tailed it out of there as soon as he left the next morning.”

“And you didn’t leave a note?”

"Yes, I did. I told him he was horrible and mean, and I never wanted to see him again.”

Annie tapped her fingers on the table. “But now you’ve had time to think, you realise you made a mistake? Am I right?”

Mary managed a small smile. “You’ve guessed right, Annie.”

Annie returned her smile, her eyes shining with warmth. "Well, let’s hope Evan explains what happened to Jed and Jed’s understanding.”

She stood up and walked over to the window, Mary quickly joining her.

“Oh, I wonder how long my brother’s going to be?” Mary worried.

"Well, he isn’t here yet, so I think we should carry on with preparing tonight’s meal. It’ll keep us distracted. I hope.”

Jed and Evan sat in the dimly lit inn, the piano music playing in the background and the low murmur of the clientele around them as they sipped their whiskey.

"So, Evan," Jed began, fixing him with a hard stare, "you're saying all you did was give Mary a spanking?"

Evan nodded, taking a sip of his drink. "That's right, Jed. I know it might not be the way things are done around here, but where I come from, a man's gotta keep his wife in line. And Mary, well, she was being a right sassy little thing. She slapped me around the face, and I knew the only way to calm her down was by putting her over my knee."

Jed studied Evan's face, searching for any signs of deceit. To his surprise, the man seemed genuine in his words, even a touch defensive.

"Well, I'll be," Jed murmured, leaning back in his chair. "I ain't gonna lie, Evan, I was ready to string you up for laying a hand on my sister. But if all you did was give her a good ol' fashioned spanking, well, I reckon I can't fault you for that. It’s something I totally agree with."

Evan's shoulders visibly relaxed, and he let out a sigh of relief. "I'm glad you understand, Jed. I know Mary can be a handful, but I do care for her, honest."

Jed nodded, a thoughtful expression on his face. "Well, seeing as that's the case, why don't you come back to the ranch with me? You and Mary need to talk."

Evan nodded. "I'd like that, Jed. Although I don't know how she's going to receive me."

"I think you'll find she's missing you. I know my sister."

Jed watched as a smile tugged at the corners of his lips.

"I hope so. I sure do miss her."

Jed clapped a hand on Evan's shoulder, a hint of a smile on his face. "Just so you know, if you're lying to me and you have actually hit my sister, you won't be leaving the ranch. Understand."

Evan visibly paled. "I assure you, Jed. I'm speaking the truth."

"Good to hear it." Jed downed his whiskey and stood up. "Then there's no need for you to worry. Now, let's get your things and head on back."

As the two men set off for the ranch, Jed couldn't help but feel a newfound respect for Evan. Perhaps his sister's husband wasn't as bad as he had initially thought. After all, a little discipline never hurt anyone, and if Evan truly cared for Mary, then Jed was willing to give him a chance.

The only obstacle in Evan's path now was Mary herself.

"They're here!" Annie called out.

Mary had just put the pie in the oven, and her head snapped up at Annie's exclamation, her heart racing. "They? You mean Jed and... and Evan?" She wrung her hands nervously, her eyes darting towards the door.

"I'm guessing so. Look. Is that him?"

Mary rushed over to the window and let out a shaky breath. "Oh, Annie, it is Evan! I don't know what to think. What if he's still angry with me?"

Annie placed a comforting hand on Mary's arm, giving it a gentle squeeze. "I should think he still is. Any man would be if his wife ran off like you did. But don't worry. He's here now, and you can at least talk to him. And remember, we're here to help out if you need us."

The sound of the door opening had both women turning their attention towards the entrance. Jed's voice carried through the house, followed by the equally deep timbre of Evan's.

"...and I'm telling you, Evan, you're more than welcome to stay with us for a spell."

Evan's response behind him was muffled, but the tone was one of gratitude. Mary's breath caught in her throat, and she glanced at Annie, her eyes wide.

Jed stepped inside the kitchen and looked at Mary. "I've brought your husband home. You and him need to talk, Mary, but first of all, I'd like a private word with you. I want your version of events, but this time, you're going to give me the truth."

Jed turned to Annie. "Annie, this is Evan. And Evan, this is Annie. She's helping out here for a while."

Evan shook her hand. "Pleased to meet you."

"Likewise." Annie replied. He was a handsome-looking devil, and she could see why Mary had fallen for him. "Take a seat, and I'll make some coffee."

Annie watched Jed lead Mary away into the other room, wondering what he was going to say to her. She'd love to be a fly on the wall.

She made small talk with Evan as the coffee brewed, and by the time she'd placed the cups on the table, Jed and Mary were back in the kitchen. Mary looked a little flushed, but she also appeared a lot calmer.

"I suggest you two have your coffee in the living room; we'll stay in here to give you some privacy." Jed said.

Annie quickly put two cups on a tray and handed it to Mary, shooting her a smile. Hopefully things would work out for them both.

When they'd gone, Annie sat down opposite Jed and handed him one of the steaming mugs. "It seems you two have worked things out."

Jed leaned back in his chair. "Mary would've found it much easier if she'd just told the truth. Did she tell you what really happened?"

Annie nodded. "Yep." She chuckled. "She got a spanking."

Jed's eyes sparkled with mirth. "Just as all naughty, badly behaved girls get. You should know, eh, Annie?"

"Oh, fiddly, dee! I'm not always bad. You're just a bit of an ogre."

He placed his cup down. "An ogre, am I?"

She drew invisible circles with her forefinger on the tabletop. "Well, not all the time," and then looking at him with a mischievous grin, she added, "Just most of the time!" She laughed and stood up, but he was on her in seconds, wrapping his big arms around her and stopping her from moving.

"Care to repeat that, little girl?" His breath was right by her ear, and it sent shivers of excitement rippling through her.

Her breath shortened, and she could feel every muscle, every sinew moulded to her body. It set her senses on fire, and before she knew what she was doing, she had twisted in his arms and found her lips only inches from his.

"Ogre," she whispered softly, her breath making the fine hairs on his moustache dance. She felt him go dead still, and then his eyes locked with hers, a look of intense desire appearing in their hazel depths.

She sucked in a sharp breath, and then his head dipped down as he laid claim to her lips. His kiss was demanding yet gentle, coaxing a response from her that she easily gave. She wanted this. She wanted him.

She raised her hands to clutch his broad shoulders as his arms slid behind her back to clasp her more securely to his side as his mouth ravaged hers.

His tongue slid into her mouth as his kiss deepened, and Annie couldn't help the low moan in her throat. Her senses were alive, attuned to him completely, every fibre of her being revelling in his touch.

He broke the kiss but still kept his arms around her, his mouth close to hers. "I could kiss you all night." He said, his voice low.

"I don't mind," Annie whispered, raising her mouth and grazing his bottom lip with her teeth. She felt his hands tighten on her waist, and he almost growled, "No, Annie. This ain't right. I'm a lot older than you and...

"That don't matter, none, Jed. I ain't ever felt like this about anyone. Now kiss me again."

He needed no persuasion. With his firm hands around her waist, his lips covered hers instantly, the firm flesh grinding into hers in a searing kiss. When they finally broke apart, they were breathing heavily and looking at each other with a yearning that only lovers could experience.

Suddenly the kitchen door opened, and Mary appeared with Evan. "We're back together!"

Annie rushed over to them. "Oh, I'm so happy for you both."

Jed watched the exchange, a satisfied smile on his face. "I'm glad for you. Truly I am." He looked at Annie. "Another plate for dinner tonight, Annie."

Annie smiled at him and, glancing over at Mary, said, "Well, come on, Mary, give me a hand."

Grinning at her, Mary rushed over, but Evan spoke up. "Should she be doing that in her condition?"

Jed clapped a hand on his shoulder. "Come into the living room, Evan; there are some things you need to know about women."

As their voices trailed off, Annie looked at Mary. "Is everything truly alright, Mary? Are you happy?"

Mary nodded. "More than anything. I missed him so much. I tried to pretend I didn't, but the truth was, he's a part of me now. Especially with this little one growing inside me." She patted her stomach. She eyed Annie thoughtfully. "Speaking of which, I noticed my brother's hands around your waist just now. Are you courting?"

"Oh no. nothing like that." Annie said, blushing.

"Uh-huh. Didn't seem like nothin' to me."

"Hush your mouth, Mary. You didn't see anything!"

Mary giggled, "Alright then, have it your way, but just so you know, I would welcome you as a sister-in-law."

"Ah, Mary, you're making me blush!" she grinned. "Now quit it and get that pie out of the oven!"

That night, Annie lay in her bed, the events of the day playing out in her mind. The reunion between Mary, Evan, and Jed had been a heartwarming sight, but Annie found her thoughts drifting to a more personal matter—the kiss she'd shared with Jed.

She couldn't help but remember the way his strong, calloused hands had felt on her, the warmth of his body so close to hers. Jed was a rugged, handsome man, and Annie couldn't deny the attraction she felt towards him. The age difference between them didn't matter to her. If anything, it gave Jed a sense of maturity and experience that she found incredibly appealing. But for some reason it seemed to bother him.

As she closed her eyes, Jed's face filled her mind. She remembered the way his brow had furrowed with concern, the gentle touch of his fingers against her cheek. A shiver ran down her spine, and she couldn't help but wonder what it would be like to be held in his arms again. Would he kiss her again?

She imagined Jed's lips on hers, his hands caressing her curves, the two of them losing themselves in a passionate embrace. The heat that rose to her cheeks was matched only by the fluttering in her heart. She suddenly found herself quite damp between her thighs and tried to think of something else. Anything else but Jed.

As sleep began to claim her, Annie's dreams were filled with visions of Jed—his strong, handsome features, his intense hazel eyes, and the promise of a future together that she couldn't help but long for. Maybe one day.

Chapter Nine

Jed sat at the kitchen table, his brow furrowed as he stared pensively into his coffee. The past few days had been a whirlwind, with the return of Evan and Mary and then the news of her pregnancy, but Jed found his thoughts constantly drifting back to Annie.

He couldn't deny the growing affection he felt for her. She was every bit the woman he had envisioned for a wife. Sassy, beautiful, and a fine figure as well, especially that delightful peachy little bottom he'd had the pleasure of disciplining.

Jed let out a heavy sigh, running a hand through his hair. At thirty-six years old, he'd all but resigned himself to a life of bachelorhood. But now, with Annie in his life, he couldn't help but feel a glimmer of hope. She was younger than him, and yet the age gap didn't seem to bother her. Their shared kiss yesterday had proved that.

As Jed mulled over his feelings, a sudden idea struck him. "Annie!" he called out, a smile spreading across his face.

Annie appeared in the doorway, her blue eyes bright with curiosity. "Yes, Jed? What is it?"

Jed motioned for her to join him at the table. "How would you feel about taking a trip back to visit your pa? The snow's cleared enough, and I reckon it's high time we paid him a visit."

Annie's eyes widened, and a smile appeared on her face. "Could we? That would be wonderful! I've been missing him so much, and I made a Christmas present especially for him."

Jed chuckled, "Well, then it's settled. We'll head out within the hour."

Annie grinned at him. "I'll get ready right this second!" And she was gone, like the little madam she was.

Jed leaned back in his chair, a thoughtful expression on his face. Seeing her face light up like that made him happy. He'd like to be the one that did that every damn day.

Well, one thing that would be good about this trip was that it would give them the perfect opportunity to talk properly together without having interruptions from the cooking and general day-to-day chores on the ranch.

He left the kitchen with a spring in his step, ready to get the wagon ready.

Annie couldn't hide her excitement as Jed helped her up onto the wagon seat. "Oh, I can't wait to see Pa!"

He smiled at her and tucked a blanket around her waist, his big hands sending ripples of excitement rushing through her. Trying to get her emotions under control, she snuggled into the layer of extra warmth, appreciating how thoughtful he was being. Under that gruff exterior, there truly was a man who cared a lot.

He walked around the other side and stepped up onto the seat next to her, grabbing the reins and quickly setting the horses into motion.

"I can't lie, Annie; I'm looking forward to the trip myself. It's nice to spend some time with you alone."

"Oh. Is it?" Annie said, blushing. Her thoughts turned to her naughty dreams last night, and trying to push them from her mind, she asked him about his sister.

"Is Mary going to stay at the ranch for long, do you know?"

"She hasn't said. Evan seems to be enjoying himself, but it all depends if he wants to go back to being a salesman again."

"I hope they decide to stay. I really like Mary. She almost feels like the sister I never had."

He angled his head to look at her. "You like her that much?"

Annie nodded. "We have so many things in common. She likes the same books that I do. She likes dancing." She paused for a moment. "The only thing she dislikes is sewing. But that don't matter, none. Not when I'm around because I love to make things."

"Like curtains." He said, raising an eyebrow.

Annie scowled. "Yes, like curtains."

She watched an easy smile break out on his face, and she narrowed her eyes, feeling a little vexed. "Not that you'd appreciate that."

"Now, now, Annie. I'm just having a little fun."

"At my expense." She huffed, folding her arms over her chest. "Everyone else said they looked lovely."

"And I agree, they do. It was just the way you went about it that was all wrong. But I'm sure you realise that now."

"I won't forget it in a hurry, that's for sure." She couldn't help the grimace that spread across her face when she remembered her first spanking from him. No, siree, she wouldn't forget that in a long while!

He changed the subject. "Did you mean what you said yesterday—that my age doesn't matter to you? You know, if we were to be together."

"No, Jed. It don't bother me, none."

"Well then, what do you say to us getting hitched?"

Her head shot round to look at him. "What? Just like that?"

He nodded. "I know you're a capable woman. You run that ranch like it was your own. Why, you even keep the men in line. I'd say you even enjoy it, wouldn't you?"

"Well, yes, I do, but..."

"Well then, what have we got to lose?"

She eyed him seriously. He hadn't mentioned love. "Is that what marriage is about to you?" She asked him.

He thought about it for a moment and then replied, "Yes, a big part of it..." He went to say more but suddenly stopped mid-sentence and pointed towards her house as it came into view. "Look's like your pa's had a visitor."

There was a man coming towards them on horseback, and Annie immediately recognised him. "It's Dr. Harris. Oh, Lord, I hope Pa ain't ill."

Jed pulled the wagon to a halt as he drew alongside the doctor, and Annie immediately asked, "Are you here for Pa, Doctor?"

"Morning, Annie, Jed." He tipped his hat and then looked gravely at Annie. "I'm afraid your father isn't very well, Annie. Not well at all. It's his chest." He frowned. "Your father told me you were away; are you back to stay for a while? He really needs someone to tend to him."

"Isn't Emmy here?" Annie asked.

"No, she's come down with the same thing. Your timing is most fortuitous, I can say."

Jed listened to the doctor, and his stomach dropped. "Is Abel going to recover?"

Dr. Harris nodded. "With the right care, I'm sure he will. He gets a bad chest most winters, but this one seems a might worse than previous years. Annie knows what to do though, don't you?"

Annie nodded, her small face looking worried. Jed reached for her hand and squeezed it gently. "He'll be fine, Annie."

"You don't mind me staying?" She asked, her big blue eyes looking troubled.

"I wouldn't expect you to come back. Not until he's back in good health. You stay as long as you need."

He noticed she visibly relaxed. He nodded to the doctor. "Thanks, doc."

"If you need me, just send word. I'll come by tomorrow anyway to see how he is."

Jed set the horses in motion and stationed the wagon out front. He jumped down first, and then, putting his hands around Annie's tiny waist, he helped her down to the ground. She smiled up at him, her eyes soft. "Thank you for being so understanding, Jed."

Brushing her skirts down, she hurried to the front door and stepped inside the house. Jed followed right behind her. They both kicked their boots off and headed into the living room.

Her father was sitting by the fire, wrapped up in a big blanket. His face lit up with joy on seeing them, and then he tried to stand up. In the process, he gave a deep, rattling cough.

"Pa! Sit down! You're not well!" Annie exclaimed, rushing to his side and guiding him back down into the chair.

"Oh, t'ain't nothin' I haven't experienced afore, Annie. Quit fussing."

Although he said the words, Jed could tell that he was pleased to have her home. It was written all over his face.

Annie glanced around the room. "I'm pleased to see everything tidy, Pa, and at least you have the fire going. Was that down to Emmy?"

"She's been checkin' in on me every day, but now she has the same dang thing. Maybe yuh could check in on her for me later? Make sure she's nice n' warm."

Jed cleared his throat, drawing the older man's attention. "Seems like it might be a lot easier if she moved in here with you for a spell." He gestured to Annie. "It'd mean Annie wouldn't have to venture out on her own."

Annie turned to Jed, her expression appreciative. "That makes a lot of sense." Crouching down next to her pa, she patted his hand. "What do you say, Pa? Shall we go and fetch her?"

"As long as yuh don't mind lookin' after us old pair of fools, Annie."

Annie laughed. "Nothing would give me more pleasure, Pa."

"Well, then, we might as well go now, Annie." Jed said to her, "Get her settled in before I head off back to the ranch."

They left Abel and headed back outside to the wagon. As Jed helped her up onto the seat, she looked down at him. "Thanks for helping out, Jed. I don't know what I'd do without you, to be honest."

He smiled, "I know very well what you'd do, little girl—everything you shouldn't." He hopped up onto the bench next to her and took hold of the reins. "You'd be traipsing out in that snow with no thought for yourself."

Annie bristled a bit but then realised he was most probably quite right.

"That's why you need to marry me. So I can keep an eye on you." He said matter of factly.

She gave him a sideways glance, deciding that now wasn't the right time to give him her answer. He didn't seem to expect one either.

Anyway, she was too worried about her pa to even think about marriage at the moment. The wagon trundled out of the gates, and Annie directed Jed on which route to take.

A little while later, she said quietly, "Are you going to be alright at the ranch, Jed? I can't help feeling I'm leaving you shorthanded."

Jed's brow furrowed, and he fixed her with a stern look. "Now, Annie, I know full well you've got a contract to fulfill, but your place is here with your pa, and you know it. You also know that even if I begged you, you wouldn't leave your pa alone."

"I know, but I just feel..."

He interrupted her. "Well don't! When he's recovered, you can come back, but not until then, do you hear? Besides," he continued, his expression softening, "I have Mary and Evan to help out now. So take your time, and when you're ready, I'll come and get you."

His words made Annie feel a lot better. "Thank you, Jed. I promise, I'll send a message as soon as I can."

Jed nodded, a hint of a smile tugging at the corners of his lips. "I'll be waiting for it, Annie."

They arrived at Emiline's, and Annie knocked on the front door. When there was no answer, she knocked again, and this time she placed her ear to the wood. She heard a weak voice call out, "Come in."

Quickly, she opened the door, and they found Emmy huddled in a blanket, sitting at the kitchen table. She didn't look at all well but managed a weak smile and croaked, "Annie, dear. It's lovely to see you." She looked at Jed enquiringly, so Annie quickly introduced them.

"This is Jed Wheeler; he does business with Pa."

She narrowed her eyes. "Wheeler? Ain't you that varmint that's been hassling Abel?"

Jed grimaced and scratched his head. "When you put it like that. I guess so."

Seeing his discomfort, Annie stifled a smile and said quickly, "That's all sorted now, Emmy. Everything's fine. It's just you we need to worry about at the moment."

"I'm doin' fine, Annie. Have you been to see your pa?"

"Yes, and he agrees with us that we should bring you back to my house. I can look after both of you then."

"Oh, I don't need no lookin' after, Annie."

Annie shot her a look of exasperation. "Yes, you do. Anyhow, I ain't taking no for an answer. There's plenty of room, and you'll be nice and warm. Besides, you like my cooking."

Emmy nodded slowly. "Well, if'n you're sure?"

"I am!" Annie said decidedly. "Shall I go and pack some things for you?"

Half an hour later, they set off back to Annie's homestead. Jed had made sure to wrap both of them up against the cold, something Emmy had remarked upon. Saying what a fine gentleman he was.

Annie laughed under her breath. How quickly he had gone from being a varmint to a gentleman.

Back home, and with Emmy and her pa sitting by the fire, Jed drew Annie into the kitchen, out of sight.

"Now, I'm gonna leave, but I'll drop by in a few days to see if you need anything. Do you want me to send one of the boys round to stay? Help out a bit."

Annie shook her head. "No, Jed. Honestly, I'll be fine. The doctor's coming tomorrow, and if I need any help, I'll let you know."

"Well, if you're sure." He placed his hands around her waist and drew her to him. His hazel eyes looked intently at her, and Annie felt her heart skip a beat. She'd got used to being around him in such a short space of time that now it felt unusual for him to leave.

"I'm going to miss having you around, little girl." He said, echoing her thoughts. He dipped his head and placed his mouth over hers gently at first, and then when she responded, his kiss deepened. When his tongue slid into her mouth, Annie felt her legs grow weak and moisture gather between her thighs as he set her senses on fire.

She raised her hands to clasp his muscular shoulders, loving the feel of his masculine strength beneath her fingertips. She felt so small against him and secure.

He broke the kiss and murmured against her lips. "Think about getting wed, Annie. I'd make you a good husband. You wouldn't want for nothing."

She lay her head against his chest, hearing his steady heartbeat, and said, "I will, Jed, I promise."

"That's good enough for me, Annie. Now, I'll take my leave, but remember, you want anything, anything at all; you send word; do you hear?"

"Yes, Jed." She stepped away from him reluctantly, and he walked to the door, pulled on his boots, and with one last lingering look, he was gone.

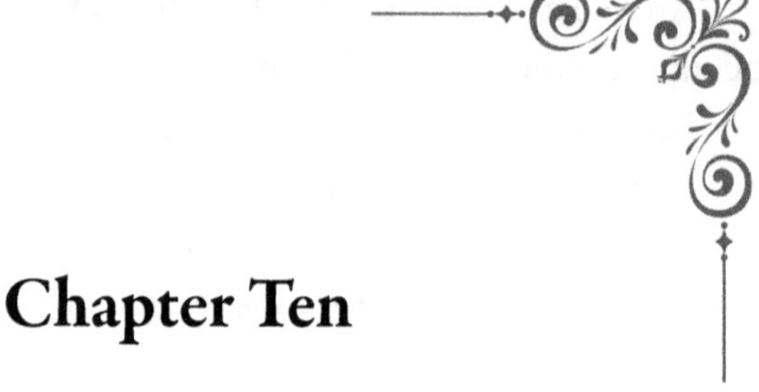

Chapter Ten

Jed awoke with a start, the familiar surroundings of his bedroom doing little to ease the heaviness that had settled in his chest. As the fog of sleep cleared, the realization hit him—Annie wasn't there. His little girl—as he now thought of her.

Letting out a heavy sigh, he rose from the bed and began his morning routine. The usually comforting task of washing and dressing felt hollow without Annie's warm presence nearby. Her infectious smile and cheerful humming had become such an integral part of his day.

He made his way to the kitchen, the aroma of cooking food wafting towards him. It seemed like Mary was doing her bit to keep the ranch hands fed, so that was something.

He sniffed the air. It didn't smell too bad, and most of the ranch hands would eat anything within reason. He stepped inside to see Mary bustling about, her brow furrowed in concentration, as she prepared the breakfast.

He took his usual seat and glanced at the men, who were seated at the table. Danny was eating a plate of what looked like scrambled eggs with black bits in and was grumbling under his breath. Marvin was sipping on a cup of coffee, his face wincing as he swallowed.

Billy glanced at him and muttered, "I sure do miss Miss Annie's cooking."

Mary whirled around and placed her hands on her hips, fixing them with a stern glare.

"Now, y'all listen up," she said, her voice sharp. "I know I ain't no Annie, but I'll thank you to keep your complaints to yourselves. She's tending to her pa. So you'll just have to put up with my cookin' for now. And if you don't like it, you can skedaddle and eat nothin'!"

Jed laughed under his breath and clearing his throat, he said, "Now, now, let's not get too worked up here. We know you're doing your best, Mary, and we all appreciate it, don't we, boys?" He looked around at his men with his eyebrows raised meaningfully.

The ranch hands murmured their apologies, and Mary's shoulders visibly relaxed. The last thing Jed needed was for her to have a hissy fit and not cook at all. Something was better than nothing!

When she turned her back to resume cooking and was moving the pots and pans around, Jed addressed the table. "I know it ain't the same without Annie," he said, his voice low. "But she'll be back before you know it. In the meantime, just deal with it."

They nodded in unison, and taking a deep breath, Danny raised his fork to his lips and began to polish off his scrambled eggs.

Three days passed, and Jed hadn't heard anything from Annie. Which was good news, he guessed, as she would have sent for help if she needed it. But he still couldn't stop feeling worried. He was also missing her more than he cared to admit.

Calling out to Marvin that he'd be absent for the afternoon, he left him in charge, saddled his horse, and set out for Annie's homestead.

The snow was still lying on the ground, but it was nowhere near as thick as it had been, so even though it was cold, at least he could still travel. He looked across the fields, enjoying the scenery as Nyx walked steadily along the path.

As the familiar little house came into view, Jed's eyes immediately landed on Annie, perched precariously atop a rickety ladder, hammer in hand.

Kicking Nyx into a canter, he came to a standstill right near her. "Annie!" he called up. "What in the blazes do you think you're doing? Get down from there this instant before you break your neck!"

Annie paused, glancing down at him with a startled expression. "Jed? What're you doing here? I thought you weren't coming for a while yet. I'm just trying to fix a hole in the roof before Pa wakes up."

Jed shook his head and quickly dismounted. "I don't care if the whole dang roof is falling down; you get your stubborn self down that ladder right now, you hear?"

Annie opened her mouth to protest, but Jed cut her off, his voice stern.

"I mean it, Annie. If you don't get down this instant, I'll tan your hide so hard, you won't be able to sit for a week!"

Annie's eyes widened, and she glanced nervously towards the house. "Jed, please, you'll wake Pa!"

Jed's jaw tightened, and he fixed her with an unyielding stare. "I don't care who wakes up, Annie. You get down here, and you get down here now, or so help me, I'll come up there and drag you down myself!"

Annie hesitated for a moment, and he watched the play of emotions cross over her face. Finally, with a reluctant sigh, she began to carefully make her way down the ladder, her movements slow and cautious.

As her feet touched the ground, Jed strode over to her. "Now, you listen to me, little girl," he said, his voice low and serious. "I won't have you taking unnecessary risks. The only thing you need to be doing is taking care of your pa—not climbing up on ladders and breaking your neck!"

Annie opened her mouth to argue, but Jed raised his finger in warning, "Don't even think of arguing back! You know I'm right.'

She looked at him mulishly. "I'm quite capable, Jed. You're being far too cautious."

Jed let out an exasperated sigh, and placing his hand on her chin, he raised her face to his. “One more word, and I’ll take you straight into the barn and warm your bottom. What’s it to be?”

Her eyes widened a little at his threat, and he watched her cheeks flush hotly, but she wisely chose to hold her tongue. She knew he was deadly serious.

Softening his expression slightly, he said. "I know you’re capable of many things, Annie, and I can understand you wanting to help, but your safety is what's most important to me right now. Understand?”

She nodded. He could tell by her whole demeanour that she wasn’t happy with being told off but

then she shouldn’t be climbing ladders. He dropped his hand and then asked, “Now, how's your pa doing?”

“Much better. The doctor came yesterday and listened to his chest. He said he’s improving already.”

“And Emmy?”

“She got better the day after you left. I ain’t ever seen anyone recover so quickly.” She laughed and shot him a wicked smile. “Although she seems to like staying here, so I don’t reckon she’ll want to return home anytime soon.”

“How does your pa feel about that?” He laughed.

“I reckon he’s sweet on her. I really do.”

He reached for Annie and put his arms around her waist. “Same as I am about you.” He watched the colour rise in her cheeks, and her eyes sparkled with happiness.

“Is that so, Jed Wheeler?”

“Yes, it is, little girl.”

Annie listened to the deep timbre of his voice, and it sent shivers of excitement down her spine. Sliding her hands up his chest, she laced her fingers together behind his neck and, reaching up on tiptoes, placed her lips near his.

"Well, then, I guess you'd better kiss me."

"Oh, I intend to." He growled, and without hesitation, his lips captured hers in a searing kiss.

Annie surrendered to him; how could she not? He was everything she desired, and being apart from him for the last few days had made her realise that more than anything.

His kiss deepened, his tongue sliding into her warm depths, demanding her response. She inhaled his scent—a mixture of woodsmoke and leather—and revelled in the feel of his massive arms wrapped around her. Oh yes, she had most definitely missed him.

They broke apart a little while later, but he kept his hands on her waist. Up so close she could see the golden flecks in his eyes and found herself almost spellbound. He smiled at her, an easy smile that warmed her heart.

"I've missed you, Annie." He ran a finger down her cheek, his eyes searching hers. "When do you reckon you'll be able to come back to the ranch?"

"Well, the way Pa's improving, I reckon in a few days. Dr. Harris is coming again tomorrow, so I'll see what he says." She placed her small hand in his. "Come inside and see for yourself."

They walked to the front door, and Annie showed him inside. Shrugging off their jackets and boots, she led him into the living room. Her pa was playing cards with Emmy, and they were both thoroughly engrossed.

"Pa, Jed's here." She announced.

Her pa looked up and smiled, "Jed, take a seat. Do you fancy a game?"

"I won't if you don't mind. I just came to see how you were." He looked at Emmy and said, "And you, ma'am."

"I'll go and make us some coffee." Annie said as Jed settled himself on a chair next to her pa. She left them to talk and bustled into the kitchen.

It felt so good to see Jed again. She'd thought about his marriage proposal a lot over the last few days, and seeing him again and the way he made her feel made her realise that her heart was already lost to him. But she had always wanted to marry for love, and that meant love coming from both sides. Did he love her?

The way he looked at her like he could eat her up certainly said a lot. But was that just lust? Oh, dang. She was so confused.

She tutted to herself and set about making the coffee.

Jed left the homestead after kissing Annie thoroughly and headed for home. She was a fine woman. A fine woman indeed. She'd make the most perfect wife, but he hadn't pressed her for an answer yet. He'd wait until her pa was recovered and she was back on his ranch before asking again.

Smiling happily, he trotted out of the gate, and it wasn't until a full ten minutes later that he realised his hands were cold. He looked down and groaned as he realised he'd left his leather gloves behind.

"Dagnabbit!" He swore loudly and pulled on Nyx's reins to bring him to a standstill.

Did he need them? Could he do without them? No, he damn well couldn't. His other pair were worn and offered no protection against the cold.

"Come on, Nyx, back we go."

Thankfully, he wasn't far away. Ten minutes later he steered Nyx through the gate, and within seconds his blood began to boil. For who was up on the roof, fixing the damn leak but the sassy, defiant little baggage, Annie Johnson!

"*Annie!*"

Annie was so engrossed in hammering the nail into the bit of wood that at first she didn't hear Jed at all. But then, as she leaned back to admire her handiwork, she heard his bellow. She froze, her eyes widening. Oh, Lord. Oh, No!

She looked down from her lofty vantage point to see his eyes blazing fiercely up at her and his hands on his hips.

What on earth was he doing back here? Now she was in for it!

"Get down here this minute!" He bellowed.

She thought about trying to slide down off the other side, but for one, it would be too dangerous, and secondly, he'd catch her and make her punishment even worse. Because one thing she knew about Jed was that if she misbehaved, he would carry through with his threat.

"I'm only coming down if you promise not to spank me!" She shouted down.

"Don't make me have to come up there and get you!" He warned.

Annie's buttocks clenched with dread. It didn't look like there was any way out of this. If only she'd waited until tomorrow, but then why on earth had he come back? Maybe she could get down the ladder and make a run for it. She looked down to see where he was positioned, and then she reluctantly shimmied down the ladder. Just as she reached the bottom, she jumped as far away from him as she could and started to run.

But she didn't reckon on how agile he was. Within seconds, he had her captured in his massive arms. She struggled to get away, and he pulled her close, growling in her ear. "And where do you think you're going?"

"But Jed..."

"But Jed nothing. I told you what would happen if you disobeyed me."

"Oh, this ain't fair!" She struggled again, and he gave her a hard smack on her bottom, making her yelp. "*Ouch!*"

He maneuvered her towards the barns, and no amount of digging her heels in made even the slightest difference. He was far too big and strong.

"I hate you!" She spat.

"No, you don't. You just hate that I caught you misbehaving and the fact that I'm gonna tan your backside."

"*Oooooh!*" She moaned, trying to break free again, but before she knew it, she was thrown over his lap as he settled himself on one of the hay bales inside the barn.

She kicked her legs and cussed at him, but regardless, she felt her skirts thrown over her back, her bloomers parted in seconds, and then his hard palm impacting on her backside.

She squealed and yelled, her small fists trying to hit his legs, completely furious that once again she was in his bad books, but his hand kept falling, the loud smacks filling the air and echoing around the barn. She narrowed her eyes. She'd bet he was enjoying this! He did it so often. Who was he to tell her what to do?

"*Aooooow!*" She wailed, closing her eyes, her face screwing up with the pain. "This ain't fair!"

"Fair? I told you what would happen, Annie, and you plumb chose to ignore me. You can blame this on yourself, no one else!"

Her bottom was heating up like she'd sat on hot coals, and she just knew she wasn't going to be able to sit down properly. Why did he have to have such big hands?

A few more spanks, and he finally stopped but kept her in the same position, his hand still holding her firmly in place.

"What in tarnation were you doing up on the roof again, Annie? I thought you'd finished repairing it."

"Well, I hadn't. You don't know everything."

He gave her a hard smack on her sit spots, and she sucked in a breath. "*Oh!*"

"Don't take that tone with me!" He warned her, "Why didn't you tell me there was more fixing to do when I was here earlier? I could've got up there for you."

"I didn't like asking."

He moved his hand from her back and quickly lifted her up, sitting her on his thighs so he could see her face. She winced as her tender buttocks chaffed against his trousers, but he paid no heed.

"Annie, you must learn not to be so independent. Do you hear? I'm not having you do anything like this again. I'll take my belt to you next time."

His expression was quite fierce, and Annie's eyes widened. She gulped. Lord, she didn't doubt him either.

"I'm sorry, Jed." She said in a small voice.

"So you should be, little girl. I won't have my future wife putting herself in danger."

She tilted her head. "I haven't said yes yet."

"You will." He leaned her back in his arms and kissed her soundly, his firm lips meshing with hers, making sure she was in no doubt as to how he felt about her. He pulled away, leaving her quite breathless.

He looked her deep in the eyes and said, "Now, I'm gonna fetch my gloves, which was the reason I came back in the first place, and you, little girl, are going to go back indoors and behave. Do you hear?"

"Yes, Jed." She resisted the urge to roll her eyes, and when he stood her up in front of him and offered her his hand, she took it. They walked back to the house, and when he had located his gloves, he gave her one last lingering kiss and said one word, "Behave!"

Annie watched him go. He cut a fine figure on his powerful horse, and even though she hadn't given him her answer, she knew she was going to marry him.

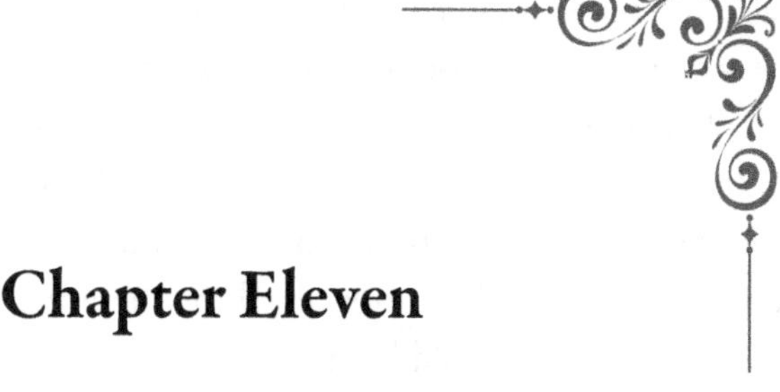

Chapter Eleven

The next day, Annie's worry for her father's health slowly began to ease. With Emmy back to her usual good health, she helped out with all the chores she could. She was a lovely woman, and watching her pa and her together gave Annie a warm glow.

When Dr. Harris stopped by the homestead, Annie seized the opportunity to speak with him out of earshot of her pa.

"I can't thank you enough for all you've done to help Pa," she said, her voice tinged with gratitude. "But do you think it'll be alright for me to leave him for a while now?"

"Absolutely. Your father's health has improved greatly, and with Emiline here to assist, I don't think you have to worry."

Annie's face lit up with relief. "Oh, I was hoping you'd say that."

"Are you returning to Jed Wheeler's ranch?" He asked her, packing his bag up and reaching for his coat.

"Yes. Why?"

"I'm going past there this afternoon; I can give him a message if you like."

"Oh, if you don't mind, that's so kind of you."

She quickly wrote Jed a note, telling him she'd be ready in a couple of days. That way she'd have time to make sure Emmy was happy with everything. Then she could leave without worrying.

She folded the note and handed it to Dr. Harris. When he'd departed, she set about making dinner, but her mind was on Jed. Humming happily, she busied herself around the kitchen, trying to keep her mind occupied—anything to stop daydreaming about the big bear of a man that would hopefully soon be her husband.

The thought made her pause half-way through chopping a carrot. What would it be like to share a bed with him? She didn't know much about what happened between a man and a woman. She had a fair idea. Over the years, she'd heard a few things here and there, and her mother, God bless her, had told her to just let the man lead the way and not to worry about anything. That didn't tell her a whole lot.

Well, there was one woman that knew what happened between the sheets, and that was Jed's sister. As soon as she got back, she was going to ask her to explain it all.

"What're you thinkin' about, Annie?" Emmy said, catching her mid-pause as she bustled into the kitchen.

Annie flushed a little. "Oh, nothing much."

Emmy gave her a knowing smile. "Is that *nothin' much* about six feet four with a smile that would melt the hardest heart? Hmmmm?"

Annie chuckled. "You don't miss much, do you, Emmy?"

"Uh-uh. I was young once, and I know that look on your face, girl." She grinned. "Does your pa know?"

Annie shook her head. "No, I ain't said nothing yet. I want to be sure before telling him."

"I've seen the way Jed looks at you. He's fallen for you; there ain't no mistakin' that."

Annie felt a warmth rush through her, and grinning happily, she resumed chopping the carrots while Emmy set to on the potatoes. When everything was simmering away, she followed Emmy into the living room and sat down opposite her pa. He was reading a book and looked up at her as she spoke. He looked so much better; his eyes were bright and free of pain.

"Pa, Dr. Harris says he reckons you're well enough now for me to go back to Jed's ranch. You alright with that?"

"Yes, Annie. I'm in fine fettle, thanks to yuh and Emmy. And the sooner yuh get back to Jed's, the sooner yuh can come back. Get this debt paid off and start afresh in the spring."

"I can stay if you like." Emmy suggested, her cheeks a little flushed. "I've enjoyed stayin' here, and it'd be nice to spend the rest of winter with you, Abel."

Annie hid a smile as her father cleared his throat and shifted in his chair. "Well, I've kinda liked havin' yuh stay here, Emmy."

"Well, that would put my mind at rest, I can say," Annie declared, standing up. "I've sent a note to Jed to come and fetch me in two days, so that'll give me time to make sure you're both settled."

"You're a fine daughter, Annie." Her father smiled at her.

"Thanks, Pa."

She returned to the kitchen, feeling relieved that she could go back to Jed's safe in the knowledge that her father would be well looked after. Emmy made a mean beef pie, one of her pa's favourites, so she knew she was leaving him in good hands.

Two days later

When the sound of a familiar wagon drew near, Annie rushed to the door, her eyes shining with excitement. But her face instantly fell when she realised it wasn't Jed who had come to collect her but Billy. Her bottom lip pouted. Why hadn't Jed come?

Billy greeted her warmly when she opened the door, and she did her best to smile brightly, even though she was disappointed and, to be honest, a bit vexed. She'd dressed so prettily today as well.

"Howdy, Miss Annie."

"Hello, Billy. I wasn't expecting to see you; I thought Jed was coming."

"Oh, he was gonna but Adeline Merryweather dropped by, so he asked me to come."

A rush of jealousy ripped through Annie, and she did her best to quell it. "Who's she?"

"Oh, she's the Marshal's niece. Fine lookin' woman. A bit hot-headed but pretty all the same." He looked down at her bags. "That all the stuff you're bringin'?"

Annie gave him a tight-lipped smile, "Yes, that's all."

He put the bags on the back and then helped her up onto the bench seat. "Put the blanket around yuh, the wind's a bit strong out on the plains."

She did as he advised and wrapped it over her lap and midriff, quickly thrusting her hands into her muffler. She closed her eyes for a moment, trying to get her temper under control. Her excitement had all but disappeared, and now she just wanted to hit something. Or someone. Namely Adeline Merryweather.

She opened her eyes as Billy set the horses in motion, and she turned to wave at her pa and Emmy, who were waving from the window. She'd already said her goodbyes indoors, telling them to stay inside, in the warm.

As the wagon trundled out towards Jed's ranch, Billy made small talk, and she did her best to respond, but her mind was on Adeline and what she'd like to do to her! Gritting her teeth, she battled to get her emotions under control before they reached the ranch.

"Billy, why is Adeline Merryweather at the ranch? I ain't seen her there before." Annie asked, trying to keep her tone casual.

Billy glanced at her, a sheepish grin on his face. "Ah, well, she don't come round often, but when she does, she makes these big doe eyes at Jed. She's mighty interested in gettin' to know him better. Reckon she has her heart set on marryin' him."

Annie felt a sharp pang of jealousy, but she quickly pushed it aside. "I see," she murmured, her gaze fixed on the road ahead. So she was after Jed. But how did he feel about Adeline? He surely couldn't feel the same as he did about her, unless he was a double crossing varmint! No. Surely not?

Suddenly, the wagon lurched, and Annie gasped, clutching tightly onto the side as a jolt hit the entire frame.

"Whoa, there!" Billy cried, struggling to maintain control of his two horses, who were just as startled as they were themselves.

The wagon came to a halt, and Annie exclaimed, "What in tarnation did we hit?"

Billy jumped down and walked back up the path. He looked down with his hands on his hips and called back, "A great big stone!" He kicked it angrily with his boot, sending it shooting off the main path into the snow. "Dang!"

He walked back and examined the wagon, muttering under his breath.

"Is it damaged, Billy?" Annie asked.

"Reckon so. The axel's bent a bit. Looks like we're gonna have to fix this before we can get back to the ranch," he said, surveying the damage. He walked to her side of the wagon and looked up at her. "Can you give me a hand, Miss Annie? I don't like askin' but it ain't a job for one person."

With a resigned sigh, Annie shook her head. "Of course I don't mind, Billy."

He helped her down, and she walked with him to see the wheel at an odd angle.

"Oh, can we fix that?"

"Sure we can." Billy said confidently. She watched as he rolled up his sleeves, fetched a box of tools from the back, and got to work.

"If you can just hold this steady, Miss Annie, I can adjust this part." Annie rolled up her sleeves, drew off her gloves, and did as he said, her nimble fingers guiding the repairs as he asked. It was hard work, but half an hour later, Billy smiled.

"Reckon that'll do it, Miss Annie." He glanced at her and then chuckled. "You've got dirt on your face."

Annie grimaced and looked down at her hands. They were smeared with grime as well. Her gaze travelled further down to her pretty dress. It was a mess, having become soiled whilst bending down on the ground and reaching beneath the wagon.

"Oh, dang! Look at the state of me!"

"Ah, don't worry none, Miss Annie. You can clean up just as soon as we get back."

Billy was missing the whole point, of course. She had wanted to look pretty and sweet for Jed, and now she looked like she'd been toiling in the fields. Oh, well, there was nothing for it but to grin and bear it. Ain't nothing else she could do.

By the time they reached the ranch, Annie was feeling really grumpy. She knew she looked a sight. As Billy helped her step down from the wagon, she caught a glimpse of a well-dressed woman staring out of the window. Her eyes were fixed on Annie, and she had an amused expression on her face.

Annie bristled immediately. That had to be Adeline. What irked her even more was that Billy had been right—she was very pretty.

The front door opened, and Jed appeared, a big smile on his face. "Annie!" He strode over to her and then stopped, looking her up and down. "What in tarnation happened to you?"

"We hit a stone, Jed." Billy interjected. "Damn wagon nearly went over, but with Miss Annie's help, I managed to fix it. She's as good as new." He said, patting the wagon.

"Unlike me!" Annie huffed.

Jed chuckled. "Ah, you still look beautiful, Annie. Come on, come inside, and get cleaned up. I've got a visitor I want you to meet."

Well, I don't want to meet her, Annie thought, her lips tightening. Sucking in a breath, she followed after him.

As soon as her eyes settled on Adeline, Annie decided she didn't like her. Not one bit.

Before Jed even had a chance to introduce them, Adeline tittered, "Well, well, Jed's been telling me all about you, but I must say, I didn't expect you to be quite so... disheveled."

Annie felt the heat rise to her cheeks, and she self-consciously smoothed a hand over her ruined dress. "I'm guessing you must be Adeline."

Adeline nodded, her eyes full of mischief. She looked so pretty and clean, which made Annie feel even more unkempt.

"For your information," Annie said through gritted teeth, "I had to help fix the wagon." And then changing tone, her voice sugary sweet, she went in for the kill, "And I didn't expect you to be quite so ugly!"

Adeline gasped. "Pardon me?"

"You heard me. Plain ugly!" Annie sneered.

Jed looked from one to the other and gave a deep sigh. That's all he needed—two women sniping at each other.

He crossed his arms over his chest. "Now listen, you two. You ain't even been introduced yet. Have some manners, the pair of you!"

Adeline immediately looked contrite. "Oh, you're so very right, Jed. I don't know what came over me." She placed a hand over her heart, her eyes shooting pure innocence at him.

He looked at Annie, expecting the same, only to find her eyes ablaze with anger, her lips tight. It wouldn't take much for her to explode by the looks of things. He gave her a dark look. "Annie?"

"What?" She snapped.

"I'm waiting."

"Well, you'll have to wait a long damn time. I'm going to my room!" She spun around and began to stalk off.

"*Annie!* Get back here!" He boomed.

"Go to hell!"

He watched her flounce off, his hand itching to make contact with her plump little bottom. But that would come later. Of that, there was no doubt. He turned back to Adeline.

She was staring after Annie with a devious look. Jed wasn't stupid; he knew she considered Annie a threat to their relationship, but truth be, he'd never wanted a relationship with her. She'd made it pretty obvious she liked him, but she just wasn't his type. Simple as.

Whereas the defiant little baggage that was gonna get her ass whopped was every bit his type.

"Well, perhaps you two will get along next time." He said, "I'm guessing Annie's a little tired from the journey and having to help fix the wagon."

"Oh dear me, Jed. She was very rude. Does she always speak to you like that?"

"No, but she'll be sorry she did."

"Oh?" Adeline tilted her head. "What're you gonna do, Jed?"

"Nothing that you need worry about, Adeline. Now, I'll get one of the boys to saddle your horse, and you can be on your way. Take care on the way back."

"But I thought I could stay a bit longer." She placed her hand on his sleeve. "We still haven't discussed my problem properly." He watched her bottom lip pout as she tried to get her own way.

He patted her hand. "Like I told you, Adeline. That problem is between you and your uncle. Best talk to him and sort it out."

Her eyes darkened with frustration, but she had the savvy to realise that he wasn't going to budge, so she smiled sweetly and said, "Well, I guess you're right, Jed and I do respect your opinion so."

He walked her to the door, and without asking, she looped her hand through his arm as they walked to the stables. Luke quickly saddled her horse, and Jed led the fine beast outside.

"Do you want Luke to see you home, Adeline?" he asked.

"Are you worried about me, Jed?"

"Of course I'm worried. A woman out there on her own."

She smiled seductively at him. "I like that you're worried about me, but you really don't have to. I'm a big girl; I can look after myself." She leaned forward and suddenly placed her hands around his neck and kissed him full on the mouth.

He quickly pushed her away. Hard enough to break the kiss but not enough to hurt her. "Adeline, you oughtn't to be doing that, girl."

"But I wanted to." She breathed softly.

"Adeline. That ain't no way to behave. Now get back home before you do anything else stupid."

Her brow furrowed. "I don't know why I'm wasting my breath on you!"

"Neither do I. Now, get going before it gets too dark."

He helped her to mount, and with one last petulant look at him, she left for home. He took off his hat and ran a hand through his hair. The poor Marshal must have a hard time living with such a brat. He turned to stride indoors and looked up at the house, just in time to duck as a vase flew straight towards him from the upstairs window.

It smashed onto the ground with a loud crash, and he looked up to see Annie's fiery little face glaring down at him.

"*You louse!*" She spat before slamming the window shut so hard that snow fell from the eaves.

He opened his mouth to say something, but she was already gone. His jaw tightening, he strode back indoors, threw off his boots, and headed for her bedroom.

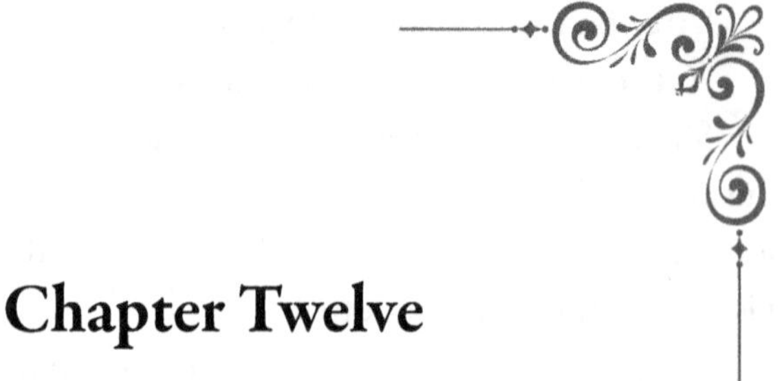

Chapter Twelve

Annie was furious. How dare he kiss Adeline like that! Right in full view of her window! What about all his sweet talk about getting married? Was it all nonsense so he could get a kiss out of her?

"*Louse!*" She shouted at the door.

She stormed around the bedroom, holding another small vase in her hand. If he dared to show his face, she was gonna throw it full pelt at him.

Suddenly the door opened, and Jed stood there filling the doorway, his face glowering with rage.

"What the devil do you think you're doing?" He said, angrily.

"What do I think *I'm* doing?" She hissed, "*You louse!*" She raised her hand to throw the vase, but she didn't get the chance. He was on her in seconds, and the vase plucked from her hands. He kept one strong arm around her whole body, pinning her to his side while he placed the vase out of her reach before dragging her over to the bed.

"You have one hell of a temper, Annie Johnson, but I have a wonderful cure for that."

She struggled to break free, but it was no use. He sat down, and she soon found herself thrown over his lap, her feet kicking uselessly in the air and her hands trying to thump his legs.

"I hate you! I hate you!" She shrieked.

"What's got into you today, little girl? You're about as bad as a brat can be."

He drew her skirts up over her back, and quickly parting her bloomers, he delivered a harsh slap to both cheeks.

"*Ooh!*" she gasped. "This ain't fair!"

"Fair? You not only spoke to Adeline rudely but also to me. You deserve nothing less, my girl."

He set up a series of quick, sharp smacks that had her wailing and hissing in pain. His hands were like goddamn shovels. No amount of wriggling or kicking stopped him.

"*Ouch! Ooof!*" She moaned, trying to break free.

Her bottom was beginning to heat up, the fiery sting making her face screw up with pain.

"*Oh!* Please, Jed! Stop!"

"Not until I think you've learned your lesson. Throwing things like that ain't how a lady behaves."

He smacked her three times in quick succession before adding, "And not to mention the way you spoke to me!" Another flurry of swats. "That was unforgivable."

"Jed! I'm sorry. Truly I am."

She wasn't gonna sit properly for weeks if he carried on, and she knew she had to apologise. She was still angry with him but if she wanted him to stop, she had to give in.

Jed paused for a moment, narrowing his eyes and looking down at her peachy little bottom, which had now turned a satisfying shade of deep rose. He couldn't help but notice the glistening evidence of her desire between her slender legs. It would seem that his naughty little girl was aroused by her spanking. Oh, how he'd love to explore her hidden treasures. But now wasn't the time.

"Are you really sorry, Annie?" He asked.

She nodded her head vigorously, and feeling she'd been punished enough, he pulled her skirts down and pulled her upwards, sitting her on his lap with his arms around her for support. He noticed her wince when her bottom touched his thighs.

Placing his hand on her chin, he made her look at him. Her bottom lip was thrust out, and her eyes still held a show of defiance.

"What's got into you, little girl? Why'd you behave like that?"

"I saw you kiss her!"

"No, you didn't. You saw her kiss me. There's a difference." She had the grace to look a little ashamed.

"But I saw your arms around her; you and her were..."

"We weren't doing anything, Annie."

"But you chose to stay with her and let Billy collect me from home. I was expecting you to come." Her bottom lip pouted.

He chuckled. "She's cunning, Annie. She said she had problems with her uncle and pleaded with me to help." He sighed. "I should've known better. It was just a ruse. I know she likes me, but I don't like her. Not in that way anyhow. Now those feelings I only keep for you."

She eyed him warily. "Do you mean it, Jed? Truly?"

He gave her a low, easy smile. "With all my heart, Annie. You're a naughty little girl, but you'll do for me. I ain't got eyes for anyone else."

Her face lit up, and she threw her arms around his neck. "Oh, Jed. I've missed you."

"Now, that's more like it." He hugged her small body to his, loving the feel of her soft warmth against him. She smelled as sweet as flowers, and he inhaled deeply, knowing how much he'd missed her. "It feels good to have you home, Annie."

She pulled back from him, raising her face to his. "Then you'd better kiss me real quick, Jed Wheeler to prove it!"

He didn't need asking twice. He lowered his mouth and claimed her lips in a searing kiss, leaving her in no doubt as to how he felt about her. She moaned deep in her throat and entwined her small hands in his hair.

He felt his cock twitch and wanted nothing more than to lay her back on the bed and ravish her, but he'd only do that when she had his ring on her finger. She was too precious to be treated any other way. He pulled apart and looked her deep in the eyes.

"Well, Annie, are you gonna marry me?" He saw a slight hesitation in her eyes and asked, "Are you still gonna deny me?"

"I want to marry you, Jed but I have to know... do you love me or are you marrying me for convenience?"

He raised an eyebrow, surprised. "Why of course I love you, Annie. Do you doubt it?"

"You ain't ever said it."

"Well, I find it kind of hard saying how I feel. Always have. But I do love you, Annie, and I'll always protect you. You must realise that."

"I believe you, Jed. Now, kiss me again so I can make sure."

He covered her mouth with his and kissed her passionately, his tongue sliding into her mouth, demanding her surrender. Her soft moans were music to his ears, and the thought of their wedding night couldn't come soon enough.

Much later, when Jed had left to help out the ranch hands, Annie bustled downstairs to begin preparing the evening dinner. She had cleaned herself up and replaited her hair. So now she looked and felt much chirpier than earlier.

Mary was already in the kitchen. "Annie, you're back. I've only just got back myself from town. Evan wanted to order some new clothes for me for when I start showing." She glanced down at her stomach and patted it affectionately. "How's your pa now?"

Annie was so glad that Mary hadn't been there earlier. She would have been mortified to know that he'd heard Jed spanking her. Even though she'd been on the receiving end herself with Evan, she'd still rather they didn't overhear her getting punished.

"He's fine now. Our neighbour, Emmy, is staying with him. She's lovely, and I think they like each other, if you know what I mean."

Mary placed some carrots and potatoes on the table, and they both began the process of peeling and chopping. It felt good to be back at the ranch. Annie felt like she belonged.

"You know we were talking about being sisters n'all—well, I accepted Jed's marriage proposal." Annie revealed to her, her eyes sparkling.

Mary put down her knife and rushed around to her, hugging her fiercely. "Oh, my, Annie! What wonderful news."

Annie licked her lips and looked at her nervously. "Mary, can we talk later, just us, together?"

"Sure thing, Annie. What's it about?"

"Well, I don't know the first thing about being married, and, you know, I thought you'd be able to tell me a few things." She flushed a little.

Mary's eyes widened. "Oh, I see. Those kinda things!" She giggled. "I can tell you a lot. After dinner, we'll go into your room and talk some."

"Thanks, Mary."

An hour later, dinner was ready, and Jed, Evan, and the ranch hands began to pile in. Annie couldn't help but notice the warm welcome she received from the men. Billy, in particular, seemed overjoyed by her return, his compliments on her cooking bordering a little on the excessive.

"Why, Miss Annie, this here's the best meal I've had in days!" Billy exclaimed, shoveling another forkful of pie into his mouth. "Ain't nothin' like your cookin', that's for sure."

Mary shot him a withering glare. "Well, I'm so glad my own cookin' ain't good enough for the likes of you, Billy," she huffed, her hands planted firmly on her hips.

Annie watched the exchange with a hint of amusement, but she could see that his remark had hurt her a little.

"Mary, I'm sure Billy didn't mean nothin' by it," Evan soothed, his voice low and calming. "He's just happy to have her back. Ain't that right, Billy?"

Billy had the good sense to look sheepish, his cheeks reddening slightly. "Sure, Evan, I didn't mean to upset yuh, Mary. Your cookin' is just fine, honest."

Mary's lips pressed into a thin line, and she shook her head, her expression softening ever so slightly. "Well, I'll thank you to keep your compliments to yourself from now on, you hear?"

Billy nodded eagerly, his eyes darting between Annie and Mary. "Yes, sorry 'bout that, Mary."

Jed sat back in his chair, watching the interaction between them all, and then satisfied that the situation was diffused, he stood up and drew Annie against him. "Well, boys, you might as well know, Annie n' me, well, we're getting hitched."

There was a moment's shocked silence, and then all the ranch hands at once started congratulating them both. When the noise had died down, Marvin asked, "Have yuh set a date?"

"Not yet, but we will." Jed replied. "And of course you're all invited."

"Hell yeah!" Luke exclaimed. "I love a good wedding."

Jack nudged him. "You might even find yerself a wife, eh, Luke?"

"No one would have 'im!" Danny ribbed him.

"I'll have a better chance than you, that's fer sure!" Luke replied, cuffing him around the head.

Jed rolled his eyes, kissed Annie on the lips, and then told the ranch hands to get back to work. "I think you lot need something to do!" He growled, ushering them outside.

Evan kissed Mary before following behind them all. When the kitchen was quiet again, Annie glanced at Mary and grinned. "What a ruckus that lot make. Come on, let's wash the dishes, and then we'll go up to my room for some peace and quiet."

Annie entered her bedroom with Mary and closed the door behind them, her cheeks flushing with a hint of embarrassment.

Mary's eyebrows rose in understanding, and she gestured for Annie to take a seat on the bed. "So, you want to know what happens between a man and a woman?"

Annie nodded. "If you don't mind tellin' me."

Mary cleared her throat, her expression turning serious. "Of course I don't. Well, you see, when a man and a woman come together in marriage, there's a certain intimacy that takes place." She paused, choosing her words carefully. "It can be a bit overwhelming, at first."

Annie's eyes widened, and she leaned in; her curiosity piqued. "What do you mean, overwhelming? What exactly happens?"

Mary's cheeks flushed slightly, but she pressed on. "Well, have you seen a man's, you know, manhood?"

Annie's eyes widened, and she shook her head. "No."

"Oh. Well, um, don't be alarmed when you do. It can look a little intimidating. But truly, it's really pleasurable." She paused for a moment, and Annie could tell she was thinking about herself and Evan.

"Anyway the man will, um, enter the woman, and they'll move together in a sort of rhythm until they both reach a peak of pleasure. It's a really pleasurable experience, but it can also be a bit uncomfortable, especially for the woman, the first time."

Annie's face burned with a mixture of embarrassment and fascination. "But it's not... painful, is it?"

Mary chewed her bottom lip. "It may be a bit uncomfortable at first, but after that, it's a truly wonderful experience. As long as the man's gentle and attentive to the woman's needs." She raised an eyebrow. "Not sure that applies to my brother though."

Annie's brow furrowed in thought. "Oh, I see. Well, he's been gentle so far. But we've only kissed."

"Ah," Mary replied with a nod. "Well, I'm sure, come your wedding night, it'll all be fine. I mean, it's a beautiful thing when shared between two people who love each other deeply."

Annie let out a shaky breath, her mind reeling with this new information. "Thanks, Mary. It's all a bit overwhelming, but I'm glad I spoke to you."

Mary smiled warmly. "I'm always here if you have any other questions."

"Are you going to stay here, Mary? You know, actually live here?" Annie asked. "It'd be wonderful if you did."

"Ah, that's a kind thing to say, Annie." She turned and walked to the window. "I do love it here, and Evan seems to like learning all the new skills that Jed's teaching him, but I'm not sure if he won't hanker after selling stuff again."

"He seems very settled. And they say a change is as good as a rest."

Mary laughed. "You're so right. Well, I think we'll stay here until the baby's born and then see what happens." She shot her a wicked grin. "Hopefully he'll stay put!"

Two weeks later

As the last of the guests departed, Jed turned to Annie, his eyes shining with admiration for the petite little woman that had agreed to marry him.

"Well, Mrs. Wheeler," he murmured, his voice low and rich, "it seems we finally have the place to ourselves." He placed his arms around her tiny waist and drew her against him, watching as her cheeks flooded with colour.

"So it would seem." She said softly, her eyes sparkling with a hint of mischief.

Jed raised his hand, tenderly caressing her cheek. "You know, I've been waiting a long time for this moment, Annie. To finally call you mine, forever."

She leaned into his touch and then, laughing, pulled away from him. "You'll have to catch me first, Jed Wheeler!"

He watched her quickly sprint towards the stairs and then disappear up the wooden steps, her light laughter diminishing as she headed for the bedroom.

Jed's expression shifted, a spark of desire igniting in his eyes. So, his little Annie wanted to play it like that, did she?

Chuckling, he quickly followed after her. He found her hiding behind his bedroom door, her eyes alight with mischief.

"Do you know what happens to naughty girls, Annie?" He growled, laughing, and captured one of her slender wrists.

"Jed! You ain't gonna spank me? Not on our wedding night!" She half protested, giggling. But he knew she enjoyed a little spanking; he'd seen the evidence himself, so who was he to deny his wife her desires? Gotta start their marriage off on the right foot, so to speak.

Positioning himself on the edge of the bed, he pulled her down over his lap and raised her skirts, and skilfully, like unwrapping the perfect present, he parted her bloomers to reveal her gorgeous little bottom.

He laid his hand on the skin and gently stroked the sensitive orbs, admiring how each buttock fit perfectly in his large hands. "Seems like I'll have to teach my wife how to behave, seeing as she's behaving like a brat."

"Jed!" She squealed and then giggled. "You're mean!"

"And she has a sassy mouth on her." He tutted loudly. "Only one way to remedy that."

He brought his hand swinging down onto her pert little derriere and heard her suck in a breath. Smiling to himself, he rubbed the same spot and then smacked her again, setting up a rhythm that soon had her squirming and kicking her legs.

Jed stopped for a moment to admire his handiwork, seeing the warm rosy glow, and then reaching up a little, he untied the fastenings and pulled her bloomers slowly down to her ankles and then off completely to pool on the floor.

It was the first time he'd seen her naked from the waist down, and it was a truly remarkable sight to behold. Her plump little bottom curved to her slender thighs and perfect calves. His gaze travelled further, taking in her pretty little ankles and feet. Beautiful. He felt his cock twitch, and this time he didn't have to quell his desire for soon, this sassy little madam would be his.

He placed his hand on the curve of her bottom, rubbing his palm over her sensitive sit spots, and then smacked her lightly again and then again, listening and responding to the small, sharp breaths she took. Slowly he moved his hand lower, running his fingers lightly over her glistening folds.

She parted her thighs and instinctively raised her bottom. Annie sure knew what she wanted. Slipping his finger between her folds, he rubbed gently over her slit until he found her sensitive little nub.

She moaned with desire, and the sound was like the sweetest music to Jed's ears. He gently began to stroke back and forth, wanting to give her as much pleasure as possible. The more aroused she was, the easier her first time would be.

Annie was in heaven. Jed's fingers were working their magic, and she could feel a heavy feeling begin, her whole body focussing on the attention he was giving to her sensitive womanhood. She moaned softly as he pushed one finger inside her and then withdrew again to slide over her little nub.

"Oh, Jed." She sighed. 'It's too good!"

"It will only get better, little girl." He pulled her up off his lap and, picking her up in his arms, he put her gently down on the bed.

Quickly, he stripped himself of his clothes. Annie watched him through heavy lids. She was so aroused now that she couldn't wait to consummate their marriage properly. He turned around, and her eyes widened when she saw the thick length of his cock.

Sitting up, she said, "Jed! I ain't ever fitting that inside!"

He laughed, and the bed dipped as he joined her, drawing her straight into his arms. "You'll be amazed at how our bodies will fit together, Annie. Now, let me take this dress off you; I'm dying to see you naked."

Annie helped him take off her dress, using his fingers to assist with the ties and buttons. She felt no awkwardness, only a deep-set desire to feel him inside her.

Throwing the dress aside, she watched as Jed's eyes swept lovingly down her body.

"You're beautiful, Annie. Truly beautiful."

She blushed a little, her eyes twinkling in the candlelight. "You ain't bad yourself, Jed Wheeler."

Gathering her in his arms, he covered her mouth with his, kissing her fiercely. His tongue fenced with hers in an erotic display of dominance, and Annie responded fervently, eager to taste the delights that Jed could give her.

He moved to kiss her neck and then lower still, trailing a line of fire down her heated skin, his tongue laving over her taut nipples, and then further still, over her rounded stomach, and then she gasped when she felt his hot breath over her womanhood.

She automatically went to push him away, but he captured her hands in his, and when his hot tongue seared her sensitive flesh, she lost all train of thought completely. He set up a steady rhythm, his tongue laving over her again and again until her whole body arched off the bed as she reached a mind-blowing orgasm.

Before she had a chance to come down, Jen raised himself above her, and she felt his thick cock at her entrance. She panted with excitement and opened her thighs wider to accommodate him.

Jed looked at her, his gaze intense. "I promise to be gentle, Annie."

Annie nodded, her eyes shining with trust. "I know you will, Jed."

He placed his hands on her hips and began to push slowly into her. At first, Annie thought she wasn't going to be able to take it, but she was so slick with arousal that his length was soon entirely inside her. She felt a full sensation and had an overwhelming feeling of belonging to him completely.

As he began to thrust his hips, she raised hers to meet him. There was no pain, only sheer ecstasy.

"Oh, Jed!" She moaned, feeling the same tension begin to build. Her body was on fire.

His large arms held her tight against him as he strove to bring them both the fulfilment they craved. Each thrust, sending her nearer and nearer to the edge of heaven.

Suddenly her body tightened, and she cried out as waves of pleasure washed over her. A few moments later, she felt Jed shudder, and then a sudden liquid heat released inside her. He buried his head in her neck and let out a guttural growl.

They lay quietly together, unmoving for several minutes, before Jed raised his head and looked down at her. "I didn't hurt you, did I, Annie?"

She smiled softly. "No, Jed, you just showed me what lovemaking feels like, and it was beautiful."

He rolled onto his side and brought her with him, so he could cradle her slender body against his own.

"I love you, Annie," he said softly, his voice thick with emotion.

Annie grinned and laid her small hand on his cheek. "And I love you, Jed Wheeler, with every fiber of my being."

As they drifted off to sleep, Annie had never felt more cherished, or more complete, than she did in Jed's arms—the big bear of a man that she could now call her husband.

The end

About the Author

Maryse Dawson was born in England but now lives in western France with her family - a husband, three children and two cats. When she's not writing she spends her time visiting the beaches and surrounding countryside. She has always enjoyed reading romances and loves history so began writing a few years ago to include domestic discipline in her stories. An alpha male - a feisty woman and adventures that will keep you turning the pages!

Read more at https://www.facebook.com/maryse.dawson.5.

www.ingramcontent.com/pod-product-compliance
Lightning Source LLC
LaVergne TN
LVHW050558160826
845677LV00011B/2355

* 9 7 9 8 2 3 0 8 7 1 3 8 5 *